Nights I Dreamed Of Hubert Humphrey

Daniel Mueller

OUTPOST
19

Outpost19 | San Francisco
outpost19.com

Mueller, Daniel
        Nights I Dreamed of Hubert Humphrey /
        Daniel Mueller.
        ISBN 9781937402495 (pbk)
        ISBN 9781937402501 (ebook)

Library of Congress Control Number: 2012923465

cover image: *McCall's Book of Modern Houses*

OUTPOST
     19

PROVOCATIVE READING
SAN FRANCISCO
NEW YORK
OUTPOST19.COM

Also by Daniel Mueller

HOW ANIMALS MATE

DAN J. Mueller
1801 Indiana St. NE
Albuquerque, NM 87110-6919
505 - 401 7342

For Michelle and Lili
and in remembrance of my dad
James M. Mueller, M.D.
(December 4, 1933 – February 18, 2012)

Acknowledgements

Stories in this collection originally appeared in *The Cincinnati Review*, *CutBank*, *Surreal South*, *Prairie Schooner*, *Joyland*, *Joyland Retro*, *Another Chicago Magazine*, *Story Quarterly*, *Gargoyle*, *The Missouri Review*, and *The Iowa Review*. The author wishes to thank the editors of these magazines for selecting his work for publication and the care they took with it, notably Brock Clarke, Nicola Mason, Michael Griffith, Elisabeth Benjamin, Laura and Pinckney Benedict, Hilda Raz, Brian Joseph Davis, Emily Schultz, Charles McLeod, Sharon Solwitz, M.M.M. Hayes, Richard Peabody, Speer Morgan, Evelyn Somers, Hugh Ferrer, Michael Fauver, and Russell Scott Valentino. The author also wishes to thank the editor and publisher of this volume, Jon Roemer, as well as his colleagues and students at the Low-Residency MFA Program at Queens University of Charlotte and the University of New Mexico for all the insight, support, and guidance they have given him during the drafting of these stories. He is greatly indebted to Fred G. Leebron, Michael Kobre, Melissa W. Basher, Sharon Oard Warner, Jim McKeen, Rachel Overmeir, Scott Sanders, Greg Martin, Gary Harrison, Adam Nunez, Jaimy Gordon, Steve Benz,

Cynthia Huntington, Amy Rosano, Shawn Behlen, Chris Powell, Cleopatra Mathis, Julie Shigekuni, Jack Trujillo, Marisa P. Clark, Gail Houston and Carmela Starace. The author would be remiss in not extending gratitude to the members of his own family for their patience, forgiveness, and love: Kurt Mueller, Karen Mueller-Sparacino, Shalini Shankar, Mark Sparacino, Beth Brooks, Angela Bills, and the author's mother Linda Mueller. The author dedicates this book to his wife Michelle Brooks and daughter Liliana Rosano-Mueller, without whose love the author would be truly lost.

For Jan —
With gratitude for your
friendship and understanding —
your copy of

Nights I Dreamed Of
Hubert Humphrey

Stories

by your admiring friend and teacher

~~Daniel Mueller~~

Daniel Mueller

"Then the Lord answered Job out of the whirlwind,
and said, "Who is this that darkeneth
Counsel by words without knowledge?"

The Book of Job, 38:1-2

"Anything will give up its secrets
if you love it enough."

George Washington Carver

2 That Don't Seem To Belong
in this Collection;
" Connected"
Spoils"

Notes
POV

Global—
11 Stories
7 1st person Narrator
4 3rd " "

Clowns in 3
"Pleased to Meet Me"
"Huntsville Rodeo"
"I'm OK, You're OK"

I Killed It, You Cook It

One morning after I'd gotten to my tree branch, Flaaten pulled out through the neck of his black Grand Funk Railroad t-shirt a hamburger bun bag containing a bowel movement suspended in urine. He'd tied off the bag with an electric guitar string and carried it snugly against his chest on the walk from his house to the tree and on his climb up the tree to his branch. If by then the territory we considered ours encompassed many square miles, extending from Kenny's Convenience Store to the Courtney Fields Sports Complex and from the Bush Lake ski jump to Nine Mile Creek, I had no sense of where Flaaten lived, what his home life was like, whether he had but the single half-brother stationed in Da Nong or other siblings, though in time I would learn that we'd passed through the woods abutting his back yard on numerous occasions.

"We don't want to waste this on just anyone," he said and handed me a cigarette. I took it from between his fingers and stared at it uneasily, unsure if I should put it to my lips. "Don't worry," he said and shook the hamburger bun bag so that the stool sloshed about in the liquid like a pickle in brine. "This," he said, "and that never came into contact. My method was laboratory safe. Trust me." From his blue Bic sprouted a long, orange flame, and I leaned into the airy divide that separated us to light up.

From the tree we could see the Minneapolis skyline

off in the distance, the I.D.S. Building, then in construction, a middle finger prone among others bowed at the knuckle, and the tower crane and boom that rose from the top of it in an oblong cross. As we smoked we watched cars proceed from the Crosstown Highway up Gleason Road, though none were to Flaaten's liking. When a police car turned from the exit ramp onto Gleason, he grew agitated—"Now we're talking," he said. "That's right, buddy. Come to papa. Come to papa."—and as it passed below us lofted the bag underhand through an aperture in the leaves. I held my breath as piss, shit, and trailing guitar string somersaulted through the opening on a trajectory heavenward, then earthbound and clapped on the glass beneath the greenery.

Like several of the vehicles we'd strafed in the past with tomatoes, eggs, bananas, figs, even artichoke hearts, the squad car pulled into the Chalgrens' driveway, only this time Mrs. Chalgren, who'd befriended my mother several weeks before with a tuna casserole brought to our doorstep, parted the drapes of a ground floor window and peeked out at the rotating beacon flashing red and blue. The poor dear, I thought as two police officers exited their vehicle, inspected their windshield, and, like others before them, tried to spot us through the limbs and leaves.

"What did I tell you?" Flaaten whispered. "Even Edina's finest are blinder than bats."

As if they'd heard him, the officers started toward us. Brush swished, twigs snapped. Soon the policemen were directly below us, the pentagonal crowns of their hats passing in and out of view, no bigger than trampolines seen from an aircraft.

"They were here," one said. "See that smoking butt?"

Flaaten let the butt he was smoking slip from his fingers into a tumbling free fall.

"Look, another one," said the other. "Was that even there a second ago?"

"Probably."

Between my sneakers, as if at the end of a long telescope, an eye peered up at me.

"Deliquents. Wouldn't surprise me if they set the whole goddamned forest on fire. Look at all these butts. There must be hundreds of them."

"Look up in this tree, Daryl. You see anything strange up there? Way up there in the leaves?"

"I don't see anything. Whoever they are are probably at the sports complex by now."

"You think so?"

"Uh-huh."

From then on, I believed we could not be seen, and to this day do not believe we ever really were, at least not in a way that anyone remembered. We stuck to the swamps and forests, the railroad tracks and freeway overpasses, the negative space that left no imprint on the eye. When forced by circumstance into a neighborhood, we cut through back yards, usually at a running clip, stopping only as long as it took to liberate from a garden plot a carrot, melon, or ear of corn. Things left on lawns and porches—dog leashes, coffee mugs, croquet mallets, children's toys—we gathered as we flew past and shed in the safety of a blind. We kept almost none of it, leaving the junk in cairns that marked our routes. If at day's end I was piqued by the thought of a child weeping over the disappearance of a sandbox pail, hula hoop, or Matchbox car, an adult wondering where a badminton racquet or terra cotta planter had gone, I told myself that if nature, by all accounts conscienceless, experienced neither guilt nor shame, neither would I.

Flaaten was likely a sociopath, I think now, limited in his capacity to experience feelings, others' and his own. But because I had yet to make any other friends in Edina, I assumed he was typical of boys my age there. In truth, I might as well have been a space traveler drawing conclusions about the human race based upon my observations of a single specimen. As it was, I wanted to be just like him, to grow my hair to shoulder-length and pull it in close to my temples with a blue bandana, so that the tails of the knot would flap with it when we ran. More than that, I wanted to be as affectless as he was, to approach situations with as diminished a range of reactions as his, to eliminate laughter, smiles, grins, tears from my palette of expressions and extinguish all brightness from my bearing, to be like the weather, insusceptible to emotions.

In spite of how busy my mother was organizing our household in expectation of my father's return, which she believed imminent, she noticed the change. "What's wrong with you?" she said one evening at the supper table. "You're not a teenager. You shouldn't be so sullen and brooding. I'm not ready for it."

By then it was the middle of August, and school would start in less than a week. "I'm not sullen or brooding," I replied with Flaaten's deliberateness, as if words and their meanings had to be bolted to each other before spoken.

"Look," she said, "I made your favorite dinner." She passed me the platter of tacos, prepared with corn tortillas fried in vegetable oil as opposed to the ones in tortilla shells that other kids' mothers served, the ones that came twelve to a carton and crumbled into shards in your hands.

She was right—her tacos were my favorite—but you wouldn't have known it to look at me, with my head down, regarding the fruits of her labor there on my plate as if they were no different than the Corn Nuts and Slim Jims Flaaten and I shoplifted from Kenny's Convenience Store or the cans of Hormel chili we heated over an open flame beside the railroad tracks. Flaaten valued food for its utility, the sustenance it provided when eaten or the splatter it made when launched, and was as happy to quell his hunger on a swiss chard or carrot still speckled with earth as on the cotto salami and muenster sandwiches his mother, he said, sometimes handed him as he went out the door. Usually he gave them to me.

I ate my tacos and asked to be excused from the table. "Not while others are dining, Howard," my mother replied. "It's bad manners."

My sister had eaten half of a single taco in the time it had taken me to eat three. My mother had eaten even less of hers. Leo sat in his high chair, creating abstract art on his tray out of pureed peas and yams, having ruined his appetite on breast milk.

"In case you haven't noticed," Jill said, "Mom's worried about you. Frankly so am I. You leave after breakfast and don't come home until supper. Then after supper you stay out until bedtime. Where do you go? Have you made any friends? I bet not."

"Where I go and who with," I said, "is my business, not yours."

"It is *too* my business," Jill countered. "Unlike you, I like it here. Unlike you, I've actually made some friends. Friends who don't believe you even exist and think I'm odd—me!—because I'm always talking about you."

"Darlene Chalgren came by for coffee this afternoon," my mother interjected. "She told me something very strange. She said that ever since our family moved into the neighborhood, cars have been pulling into her driveway having had foodstuffs—that was the word she used—thrown at them. I asked her did she mean tomatoes, eggs, foodstuffs commonly thrown at cars by—well, let's face it, Howard—boys your age. She nodded, but said other weirder things had been thrown from across the street as well. Figs, for instance. And artichoke hearts. And six days ago a police car had—now I know this isn't appropriate dinner table conversation, but since Darlene left, I've thought of little else—a bag of fresh human excrement land smack in the middle of its windshield."

"A bag of fresh human what?" I asked, hoping to hear her say it again, and at the dinner table no less.

"You heard me, Howard," she replied.

"Excrement," Jill repeated and nibbled her taco.

"Do you know anything about this, Howard?" my mother asked.

I said neither yes nor no. I simply did what I imagined Flaaten would do. I stared back at my mother, having rid my face of all expression and transformed it into a cypher in which she could read the answer I hoped she preferred.

"Thank heavens," she said. "I can see that you're just as incredulous as I." She laughed.

"But Howard didn't say anything," Jill bellowed. "He didn't say anything at all."

My mother shot my sister a furious stormcloud of a glance. "Darling," she said, "he just told me everything I need to know."

"But—"

"I hope you're not questioning my powers of intuition, young lady," my mother said. "Inference isn't lost on me, not when it comes to my children."

"Excrement," I said, wagging my head.

"I know," my mother said. "It's kinda funny when you take *us* out of it. I keep seeing Darlene Chalgren's face when she said it. Like she'd discovered some herself in a handsel wrapped in tissue."

The next morning I found Flaaten ammo-less, but with his wrist rocket hanging from his neck by its bands like a pair of sunglasses. He asked me whether I could see any progress on the I.D.S. Building, and I told him I couldn't. "Me either," he said, and I followed him down the tree, then through the woods past survey markers that hadn't been there the day before. Waist-high, each was topped with an orange plastic ribbon, and as we walked Flaaten yanked the flimsy wooden shafts from the ground, splintered them across a knee, and left the broken tender lying behind him in the ferns. He didn't do this angrily, but matter-of-factly, as if he and the natural world were one and he merely a thumb and forefinger tasked with removing a sliver from a nail.

Within the year this would become the Indian Hills subdivision about which my father had feigned such excitement months before, when he and my mother had first discussed moving to Edina at the supper table in Fort Hood. Try as I might to imagine the homes that would be erected on the very ground Flaaten and I treaded, it was as difficult as imagining my mother and father together in Edina at all. Though he'd promised to return to us shortly, I didn't believe him. I didn't believe for a second that his discharge was forever being postponed due to bureacratic red tape or that he had any intention of leaving Texas or the military, so perfectly, it seemed to me, had both suited him. He loved nurses, and nurses loved doctors, and while Fort Hood itself may not have been to his liking, being over a thousand miles away from my mother undoubtedly was. If familiarity bred contempt, there he could indulge his taste for the exotic without fear of reprisal, and I steeled myself against the indignation and sadness I felt on my mother's behalf even as I longed to rejoin him in Fort Hood and pretend that each new woman he brought home could, in time, take my mother's place in both our lives.

Flaaten led us through the woods down to the banks of Arrowhead Lake, a musky pond that would one day provide water views to a dozen homes. On it a couple of mallards paddled among lily pads as Flaaten put a stone in the pouch of his wrist rocket and pulled back the tapered latex tubes until they trembled as a single sinew above the long, flexed muscles of his forearm. "Please don't," I said. "Not today." With the same high-powered sling-shot, he'd taken out a squirrel and a rabbit several weeks before, game we'd subsequently gutted and skinned with a jackknife and roasted on a rotisserie fashioned out of willow boughs. I was loathe to repeat the process. But his fingers released the pouch, and as the bands snapped between the uprights, the drake squawked amidst an explosion of blood and feathers and lay quivering on the water. His mate splashed about in maniacal circles, flapping her wings and quacking, as Flaaten removed his clothes and strode through loosestrife and cattails into water green with pondweed. He swam to the dying fowl and slung it above him by its neck, droplets arcing from its webbed feet. By the time he emerged from the pond draped in watermilfoil and algae and carrying the duck upside-down by its legs, I'd made a firepit with stones pried from the marsh and lit some kindling in the center of it.

"That's a good wife," he said.

He said it without irony or spite, as if immersed in play simply acknowledging our respective roles in that day's unfolding drama. I was irked by it, but I also believed that by ignoring emotional impulses I could become more like Flaaten, whose responses to everything were resoundingly placid and objective, almost robotic. As he gutted and plucked the duck, I set up the rotisserie, using a rock to pound sturdy Y-shaped willow branches into the wet ground on either side of the firepit and whittled a skewer from a bough long enough to rest securely in the notches.

"Here you go," he said, handing the duck to me, the shiny flesh of its breasts and thighs still warm to the touch, swaddled in shredded garments of skin and fat. "I killed it, you cook it."

As the duck roasted, Flaaten squatted naked beside the fire, his drooping penis haloed by pubes as delicate and white as hoar frost. Though to my eye our organs looked virtually interchangeable, the hair surrounding his glowed as if emitting its own milky light. I didn't want to look at it. It seemed wrong to do so. And yet the color seemed preternatural there among all the greens and browns, like something that wanted notice. As the vines and clots of plantlife dried on his skin, Flaaten peeled them from his arms, legs, and chest and dropped them in the fire. They sizzled, curled into themselves, and vanished in puffs of smoke.

"Will you check my back?" he asked and displayed shoulderblades and buttocks adorned with forest green specks and tendrils.

"It's covered with seaweed," I said.

"It isn't seaweed," he replied.

"What is it then?" I asked.

"Pondweed."

I pulled off vines of it and with my fingers combed

bits of it from his hair. Then I picked wads of it from his upper back, lower back, and buttocks and flicked them onto the coals. "Thanks," he said. When the duck was blackened from bill to drumsticks, we extinguished the fire with pondwater cupped in our palms. It was too hot to eat, and even if we'd thought to bring oven mitts, there was nowhere to set it. As we waited for it to cool, Flaaten asked me if I was ready for summer to end and the school year to begin.

He so rarely asked me a question I didn't know how to answer him. "Are you nervous about it?" he asked. "Scared?"

"No," I said, though in truth I was both. I would know none of the other students except Flaaten, had known him only under cover of shade, and worried that our friendship wouldn't survive the glare of public exposure, that like an insect under a magnifying glass it would erupt into flame and expire. Though I'd moved often enough to know that one made friends wherever one went, a new kid was always viewed with suspicion, everything about him scrutinized and lambasted, from his clothing to his haircut to his accent. After four years in Fort Hood, mine was Texan twangy and already sounded funny to my own ears. "Are you?"

"Nah," he said. "School's easy. There's nothing to it. It's not like relying on your wits."

He ripped a thigh from the bird, scraped away the blackened crust, and gnawed on the tender meat beneath it. I did the same. Then we each ate a breast, a wing, and a drumstick.

Flaaten put his clothes back on. "C'mon," he said.

"Let's find some smokes." And off we went through the woods like deer veering around thickets and loping over fallen trunks on the fleetest of hooves. It was as if the duck we'd eaten had lit fuses in us both, and soon we were glorying again in our invisibility, zigzagging through back yards with arms splayed like seining nets, amassing treasure as we leapt fences and dodged patio furniture. Not until we reached Nine Mile Creek did we take inventory: a Mason jar of sun tea, lawn shears, a rake, a posthole digger, and a bra, 34 double-D, snatched from a clothesline. Flaaten always knew from whom we'd taken each item and said the name of the owner as we laid it on the mound. "Mrs. Sharpe . . . Mr. Stehley . . . Mr. Graham . . . Mr. Fulford . . . one of the Heutmaker twins, either Lavender or Sage." From his breast pocket he produced a half pack of filterless Camels and tapped out two. "Dr. Beasley." The smokes we kept, the rest we left to the elements.

It was as we were following the creek upstream to the freeway underpass that we saw the water tower, a golfball on a tee no different than others polyping the landscapes of midwestern suburbs and towns, but with its igloo-shaped door a gaping portal in its fanning base. Soon we were standing in awe before the cavity, the door that had been shut and padlocked every other time we'd gone there. Coupled to a U-bolt, the laminated Master lock we'd tried to spring over and over with rocks. Flaaten traced the threshold with his fingertips, then kicked one of the panels, and within the darkness a gong sounded. I stepped past him through the passageway into air like that of an abandoned refrigerator, though no more noxious than the gasses emitted from the stagnant pools in which Flaaten mucked. "You coming?" I called to him.

"You wouldn't get me in there if you promised me Raquel Welch, Brigette Bardot, and Jayne Mansfield naked together on a waterbed," he replied.

Beyond him mowed furrows striped the hillside to the creek and freeway where vehicles crisscrossed like targets at a shooting gallery. Everything looked different through the opening, as if I were seeing it through alien eyes.

"You're scared," I said. "You are." I was flummoxed. For the month and a half that I'd known him, nothing had scared him.

"It's stupid to go some place where you can't see what's right in front of you."

"You can see a little," I said. Welded to the primary feeder pipe a ladder disappeared into the blackness. I grabbed hold of a rung and started to climb.

"Not if someone closes the door," he said.

"You gonna do that?" I called down to him. "You gonna close the door on your wife?"

"I might," he replied.

In truth, I'd begun to hate him, and as I ascended the ladder the less significant he and all we'd done together seemed. Below me on the foundation of slab concrete sunlight winnowed until it was no brighter than a cluster of stars. Above me spanned only blackness, and as I climbed into it, I imagined my progress up the stem of a great chalice, the sheer weight of the reservoir above me a gravitational field into which I'd fallen. I could as easily have been crawling downward or sideways, my arms and legs moved so effortlessly. In time the rungs opened onto a steel latticework platform on which I stood, sat, and then lay facedown. It was a catwalk, and with my arms outstretched I could finger the edge of it, beyond which there was only air, and the feeder pipe, moist with condensation. From photographs taken later, I learned that the catwalk was surrounded by a guard rail, meant to protect those responsible for taking water samples and checking hydrostatic pressure, but unless you were standing you might roll beneath it and off. Mere feet above me, hundreds of thousands of gallons of water rested on a pedestal, and when I put my ear to the pipe I could hear water rushing through it either upward into the storage tank or downward and out to faucets and taps, I couldn't tell which.

"Come on up," I called to Flaaten. "It's better than trees, better even than the Bush Lake ski jump. It's like floating in space." No longer was any portion of the floor sunlit, though tiny perforations in the walls of corrugated sheet metal admitted tiny beams of light undetectable to the eye until retina and pupil adjusted to the darkness. When that happened, it was as if I were so far away from Earth and its problems that mine seemed sub-atomic in comparison and barely worth considering. Why fear making friends or a new start? Why fear a parent's decision to leave a marriage? Why fear anything? In an instant I thought I understood why Flaaten was the way he was. I called to him, "You've got to come up here."

"I'm here," he said, and then he was upon me, yanking my trousers down as he panted into my hair. It was all he said. I bucked and thrashed. I couldn't, obviously, *see* anything. Then it was quiet. I never even heard a thud. When I called his name, I half-expected him to holler back, "When you coming down?" or "How's it feel to be blinder than a bat?" as if what had happened had been all in my head. I pulled my trousers up. I stayed calm. I could no longer remember which direction I faced, whether the feeder pipe was to my left or right, but once reoriented I crawled backward until my feet found the opening in the latticework and then I placed them on a rung.

Going down took longer than going up. Or perhaps that's just how I remember my descent, probing the abyss with the toe of my sneaker and feeling relief when a bar withstood the weight I placed on it. The rungs were evenly separated, but each one seemed a farther drop than the one before, and when at last I stood on the concrete, I had the sensation of being as far below the ground as the water tower was above it. Flaaten had shut the door upon entering, and I shuffled toward it like a zombie, with my arms in front of me to break my fall in the event I tripped over him. I opened it and turned back around to look at him. Sunlight fell across him, his arms and legs distended as if running at the moment of impact. That would be how he'd be found several weeks later, albeit without the wrist rocket around his neck, when the water authority employee, likely the very one who'd left the door open for us in the first place, came to conduct a battery of routine quality control tests. By then, Alan Norris Flaaten had been reported missing, was thought to have run away or been kidnapped, and the discovery of his body put an end to all the endless speculation. His death was ruled a suicide, though how he'd gotten inside the water tower when the door had been "securely locked" remained a mystery.

Outside I closed the door and locked it. By then it was late afternoon and the sun was glaring. I walked past the tennis courts, skating rink and warming house to Gleason Road and followed the sidewalk past the elementary school where in three days I would start sixth grade. Then I walked past homes past which I'd soon walk every schoolday and didn't care who saw me.

Say Anything and Everything

I was in sixth grade when I first shook hands with Hubert Humphrey. My Social Studies project, a survey of voting habits conducted in the wake of Richard Nixon's landslide victory in '72, had received top honors, and Senator Humphrey, having grown up in the same small town as our principal, Mr. Moynihan, hung the medal around my neck, no doubt as a favor to his childhood friend. The award ceremony was held in the gym, and as I looked out from the stage where I'd played "Both Sides Now" and "Good King Wenceslaus" on the tenor saxophone during band concerts, it occurred to me that the senator and I were alike in a way I couldn't yet define and that the sea of humanity stretching before me from one basketball hoop to the other wasn't composed of humans at all, but something else. Automatons. Cyborgs. "People" in appearance only.

The students, seated on the floor by grade and class, formed a shadowy mosaic. Along the perimeter stood their teachers, their eyewear glinting like quarters on the eyelids of corpses. Somewhere beyond the reach of spotlights Lucas Vite squatted on his haunches, his gorgeous white hair like a swan's wings. At twelve, he was already as muscular as his fourteen-year-old brother Layne, who had been sent away to military academy for torturing neighborhood cats, and once the award ceremony was over and school adjourned for the day, he would be waiting for me in the undeveloped lots that separated his house from mine in the subdivision known as Iroquois Trail. Sitting on a garbage sack of *Playboys, Ouis,* and *Penthouses* Layne had left him in a stand of sumac, a magazine opened to the centerfold, his jeans unzipped and engorged cock squeezing out from between his bruised fingers like bread dough, he'd say nothing at all as I lay before him on twigs and leaves and, glossy pages rustling beside us on the crumpled ferns, I let him feed himself gingerly into my mouth.

"Congratulations, Jack," Hubert Humphrey said with the same wry conviction he used on the campaign trail. "I speak on behalf of your parents, teachers, and classmates when I say we are all very proud of you."

Then he gave me the smile for which he was famous, a cross between a smirk and a scowl into which almost anything could be read.

"Do you crawl home from school everyday on your belly?" my mother asked when she saw the mud and leaves dried to my jeans and t-shirt. Having returned from her job at Norquist, Lindstrom, & Norquist, where she'd recently made partner, she set two sacks of groceries on a counter that looked into a quivering canopy of elm boughs. Our home, designed by my father, was three airy floors built into the side of a wooded hill a la Mies van der Rohe's Tugendhat House.

"Shhh," I said the way my father had during stock market reports. From a bar stool I pointed at the television where anchorwoman Monique St. Croix, upon whose steely sex appeal my father had never failed to comment, was reporting on Senator Humphrey's un-announced visit to Truman Elementary.

"Hubert Humphrey visited your school?" my mother asked.

"Hold on," I said as the newscast shifted to footage of Mr. Moynihan, Hubert Humphrey, and me standing ceremoniously on the stage in the school gym, they in their dark suits and regal ties and me in clothes I hadn't yet changed out of.

"That's you!" my mother exclaimed. "What in the world . . . You have to tell me all about it. What was the occasion?"

As the 'me' on television bowed to accept the neck-band and medal, the 'me' wrapped in my mother's arms tugged the very same neckband and medal from my pants' pocket. "Remember the survey I conducted in January and February," I said, untangling myself from her embrace, "in which I collected data on the voting habits of one hundred forty-seven of our neighbors?"

She nodded, her white blond hair bearing creases from the French braid she'd worn to work.

"Well, it was awarded top honors in a special end-of-the-year ceremony."

"And Hubert Humphrey presented you the medal?"

"You saw it on TV," I said.

I'd conducted my survey to discover whether my social-scientific hypothesis—specifically, that my mother and I were constitutionally different from the other residents of Indian Hills and that this would be reflected in each respondent's choice for President

—held water. To us, George McGovern had seemed easily the better candidate. In speeches and debates he presented a cogent plan for the immediate and orderly removal of troops from Vietnam while Richard Nixon's phased withdrawal, the platform on which he'd won the Presidency in '68, had only resulted in an escalation of bombings and the miring of our nation in subsidiary conflicts in Cambodia and Laos. While during his four years in the Oval Office Nixon had dismantled nearly all of the social and economic welfare policies adopted under LBJ, vetoed nearly every piece of health and education legislation, and impounded almost all congressionally approved funds for domestic programs, McGovern promised every American an annual income, which he intended to subsidize with revenue generated by a thirty billion dollar cut in defense spending.

Of course, it hadn't helped that my mother and father's divorce had had all the nail-biting drama of a neck-and-neck race for public office, with each slandering the other so thoroughly that by the end it was difficult to believe that either was fit for parenthood. My father had accused my mother, on numerous well-documented occasions, of being a "castrating bitch," "unquenchable nymphomaniac," and "deranged psycho," while my mother had used the same occasions to accuse him of being a "philanderer," "prick," and "drunk." At the time I sided with my mother, whose assessment of my father I could corroborate with memories of him that seemed to spiral on the blade of an auger: my father's hands lifting an orange and violet paisley blouse from long, freckled breasts that dangled in the open rear window of the Volvo station wagon in which I sat, buckled in before the bare wood frame of a house being erected at the end of a secluded cul-de-sac; my father kissing a woman's neck while he showed her blueprints on a drafting table in his office below the dining room where my mother's high heels clacked across native granite; how he ogled our au pair, Simone, when she prepared me a *croque madame* and cup of tomato bisque, brought me back from a walk in my stroller, or put me down for my nap.

Iroquois Trail, a suburban subdivision that catered to upwardly mobile, two-income families like my own, took pride in the homogeneity of its International Style homes and large wooded lots. My father, who'd studied architecture at McGill on a hockey scholarship before being signed and cut by the Minnesota North Stars, worked out of our home and at construction sites inside a two-mile radius of our front stoop while my mother had to commute forty-five minutes every morning to law offices in downtown Minneapolis, where three nights a week she stayed until after Simone had read me a story and tucked me into bed. In portraits, my mother's almost pigment-less hair falls from a cupola at her forehead in porcelain shafts to the lapels of her pastel blazers, and my father's black ringlets hang as if suspended on his flaring sideburns. If both were physically stunning, I had inherited a diluted mixture of their colorings, my skin neither the olive that tanned in the summer to the brown of pecans nor the alabaster my mother protected from sunlight with parasols and creams, my eyes neither irredescent blue nor coffee, my hair a nameless hue as dull as it was course. Though by ninth grade I would shoot to a gangly six feet, at the time I was short and pudgy, and could tell by my father's sour expressions that my effeminate gestures, sprung to life on porcine digits and limbs, were repugnant to him.

I was glad when he moved out. Alone with my mother I could give free rein to the boy I was without fear of chastisement or reproach. In her company I never worried that the "I" I was would be the "I" I would forever remain. When we talked politics, which we did throughout George McGovern's futile campaign against a megalomaniac who would stop at nothing—breaking and entering, wiretapping, the nation would shortly discover—I became a version of my father that my mother could love.

"How can anyone vote for Nixon with a clear conscience?" she would ask, and I would answer, "All Nixon's supporters seem to care about is padding their bankrolls." She would nod, thinking, I hoped, of the fiscally conservative Nixon supporter with whom she was embroiled in divorce proceedings. Within a year a judge would rule in her favor, and though her six-figure salary outmatched the sizeable commissions my father received for being one of the official architects and homebuilders of Iroquois Trail, she would be handed the house we lived in plus alimony, the first of many setbacks my father would suffer on the road to financial ruin, liver failure, and death.

But on the night after my first meeting with Hubert

Humphrey, my father was very much alive, living with Simone six mailboxes down from us in one of his own glass and cedar homes.

"That Lucas Vite isn't still bullying you, is he?" my mother asked.

"No worries there," I replied with a grin. "I've got him eating out of my hand."

She sipped her scotch and replied dreamily, "Maybe one day you'll be a politician, too."

I laugh when I think how wrong her prediction turned out. I'm a systems analyst with a major multinational business machines manufacturer with offices in Hong Kong, Tokyo, London, and Phoenix. I live with my wife, Molly, and our sons Leo and Ray, ages twelve and fourteen, in a subdivision of Chandler known for its pristine 36-hole golf course and ranch-style homes abutting greens and fairways. Though I'd be hard pressed to tell a wedge from a driver, it calms me to look out cathedral windows at weeping willows draping a mountain-fed water trap stocked with cutthroat where thirty years ago malnourished goats grazed on tumbleweeds and creosote. A Minnesotan through and through, I find much of Arizona's landscape suffocating. Not so Molly, who grew up three suburbs away from me in Apple Valley and with whom I fell in love in 1986, when we attended the same "Strategic Management" graduate seminar en route to our respective MBA's. She loves it. And five days a week for the past three years has driven her cherry red Miata through it, on sunny days with the top down, to a massage therapy school in Sedona, two and a half hours away. There, in subdued environments of adobe, tile, and glass, she has learned the difference between Alexander Technique and Feldenkrais, Reflexology and Shiatsu, and become a state licensed practitioner of a form of Swedish massage that combines acupressure, neuromuscular, and effleurage therapies.

A little over a year ago when I first agreed to be her Guinea pig, Peruvian flute music encircled us. With the curtains drawn, the thermostat set at eighty, and a humidifier emitting a low but steady mantra, our den had been transformed into a sanctuary. Candles laced with aromatic oils were aflame on the coffee table, end tables, and armoire. In the center stood the massage table with adjustable face rest, a present with which I'd surprised her at the end of her first semester. "How do you want me?" I asked.

"How about on the floor with a dildo up your ass?" Molly replied. When the boys were out, as they were on this particular Saturday, horseback riding in the North Maricopa Wilderness with our Methodist Church's Youth Group, Molly and I indulged in role-play.

"I think you have me confused with another client. I'm scheduled for a straight massage. Nothing kinky."

"So sorry," she said.

Then, as if I were indeed a client and not her husband of sixteen years, Molly explained to me, as she did presumably to the walk-in traffic enticed to the school by the promise of a discounted "student" massage, that repressed, often painful memories were contained deep within the tissues of the muscles she would manipulate and that for some massage provided a powerful emotional, psychological, and spiritual release akin to hypnotic regression, intensive psychotherapy, and even exorcism. She asked me to strip down to a level of nudity I was comfortable with and informed me, as if it weren't regular supper table fodder, that she'd completed all of her class work and was a third of the way through her practicum, of which the massage I was about to receive would constitute an hour.

"Are you ready?" she asked.

"Are you?" I replied.

As Molly worked body oil into her palms and fingertips like a pitcher softening a baseball, I positioned myself face-down on the massage table, so that my arms dangled over the edges of sterilized vinyl and my forehead and cheeks rested comfortably on pads shaped like an egg but with an opening at the bottom for my chin. When she had covered me with a warm sheet, she started with my scalp and neck, and as her fingers and thumbs pried my trapezius from its housing of sternocleidomastoids, I pictured her wrists and forearms, which had more than doubled in girth since she'd gone back to school, the biceps, triceps, and deltoids that had grown rounder and more defined with each passing week. But it was funny, the more clearly I imagined my wife, the way her bra strap formed a suspension bridge between petite scapula and how her slender thighs and buttocks tightened when she pressed on me, the more she became dissociated from the physical sensations she was providing. Each muscle she massaged felt as if it were being extracted with a scalpel and forceps, and I wondered if when it was over I would be reduced to a mound of dripping viscera in a cage of bones. But even if like a coroner she were laying spinalis next to longissimus on a steel tray, I trusted her to put me back together in a stronger, healthier configuration.

As systems analysts, we had both been trained to identify and eliminate under-producing links in multinational corporate chains. Until her resignation from a competing multinational corporation, Molly had been extremely talented at cutting out unnecessary functions and streamlining management structures, such that in a decade she had saved her company tens of millions of dollars in salaries and profit sharing. But a year before she made the mid-life leap to massage therapy, she confessed to me that she believed a special ring of hell had been reserved for the likes of us, men and women who made very good livings separating other men and women from theirs. Her problem lay, I told her, in equating positions with people. If one privileged individuals over the aggregate, one threatened the entire corporate pyramid, from the CEO to regional directors to call-center personnel to mailroom staffs, employees who, like us, had families to support, mortgages to pay, futures to consider, never mind that they lived in China, Japan, or, in her case, Micronesia. Ultimately, she had to trust that she was helping more people than she was hurting.

"But I don't want to hurt anyone anymore," she said.

I was spooning her in our bed with the lights out, caressing her knee under covers of satin and down and nibbling her ear through her hair. It was August and the air-conditioner gently purred. "Nobody wants to hurt anyone, honey," I said. "But you can't take a breath these days without depriving someone of air."

"Aren't you overstating it?" she replied.

"We're going to take a financial hit."

"I know," she said.

"And what about me? Does this mean fifty years from now when we're both long dead, I'll be in that special ring of hell you mentioned with other assholes just like me?"

She laughed and faced me. "Jack, there are no other assholes quite like you."

I took it as a compliment. If at thirty-seven she had decided to put her innate capacity for ruthless incisiveness in the service of a more holistic approach to living, for one of us to wash her hands the other would have to keep his in the muck. This we understood, and as Molly unbraided cords along what I had come to learn were my seven sacred chakras, my life appeared before me as an endless corridor of past experiences, some painful, some pleasant, but most without positive or negative associations of any kind. As she unlocked memories stored in my deep tissue, I floated through a clear tube around which my days and nights spiraled like stripes on a barber pole. Everything that had ever happened to me, the significant and trivial, the memorable and forgotten, merged in the swirling maelstrom into which I was being swallowed and at the end of which, I knew even before I got there, Lucas Vite stood over me, zipping up his jeans in the woods.

His cheeks pink with shame, "Never again," he said and kicked me in the groin.

The second time I met Hubert Humphrey, my mother and I were sitting at a table in a lounge at the Minneapolis-St. Paul airport. We were flying to New York and on to London to catch a train to the Lake District, and my mother had made sure that we'd arrived for the first leg of our journey two hours prior to departure. She was nursing a Dewars, reviewing a complex, potentially lucrative class action suit against a pharmaceutical company headquartered in the Twin Cities, when I happened to look up from Larry Niven's *Ringworld*, a novel set on a manufactured, ring-shaped planet where gravity was a byproduct of centrifugal force.

Hubert Humphrey tilted his head as if suddenly under the spell of a renegade thought, spoke to a sandy-haired man on his right, then to a redhead in a lavender dress on his left. Over the shoulder of my mother's cream-colored blazer his eyes fell on me. The smile seen on newsreels lit upon his countenance, as if a fishhook yanked a corner of his mouth halfway up his cheek.

"Jack? Jack *Reville*?" he said. "Is that you? It's me, your old friend Senator Humphrey."

That quickly he was upon us. From a blue and white striped cuff a hand extended as congressional aides and Secret Service agents looked on with indefatigable patience. It was said of Hubert Humphrey that he never forgot a face, and between twelve and fifteen

I'd shed my baby fat, added twenty pounds of bone to my skeleton, and grown Mr. Hyde-like sideburns.

"It's been a long time, hasn't it?" he said. "But you know what, Jack? I haven't forgotten that survey you conducted. Brilliant work for a sixth grader. Hell, it would've been brilliant work for a twelfth grader."

My mother's tortoise shell reading glasses fell on slender chains to her gathered collar as she shut her case file.

"But everyone I surveyed," I said, "with the exception of my mother here, voted a straight Republican ticket. Everyone."

Even Hubert Humphrey's chuckle was iconic. "You did reconnaissance work for us, Jack. You showed us where we need to redouble our efforts. You can't change minds if you don't know where they are. In three years Washington's undergone a sea change. I know because I left there this morning. And I predict that by this time next year our country will have put a Democrat in the White House."

"You think so?" I asked.

"I do," he said and held out his hand to my mother. "You must be awfully proud of your son, Mrs. Reville."

"I am," she replied.

"Well, I should be going," he said. "I have meetings with my constituencies all afternoon. It was good to touch base with you, Jack. A pleasure to meet you, Mrs. Reville."

"A pleasure indeed," my mother replied.

"Bye," I said.

"Bye, Jack," said Hubert Humphrey, and with a wave

and a smile he and his entourage were gone.

"That," said my mother, "was astonishing."

My mother had booked us a cottage overlooking Lake Windermere because she had read the poems of Wordsworth and Coleridge in college and believed a landscape that had inspired some of "the most melancholy poetry ever written" might cure us of our respective depressions. Her use of the "d-word" had surprised me, and not only because her parents were third-generation Norwegians who'd passed their ancestors' agrarian contempt for the entire psychiatric profession down to her. For years I'd known she was depressed. Probably the best corporate lawyer in the country who didn't believe an ounce in what she was doing, she worked too hard, had no friends to speak of, no romantic interests. What unsettled me was that she'd arrived at the same conclusion about me. Was I depressed? For years I'd excelled at my schoolwork, had no friends to speak of, no romantic interests. Her depression I could understand. She'd chosen her arena in which to skate, and as long as she kept her fingers locked at the small of her back, manila folders containing court depositions and tort claims would span before her like groomed ice. But I'd made no such choice.

The stone cottage we'd rented might have been said to overlook the lake if one considered narrow swaths of gray through dripping black foliage a water view. My mother unpacked her attaché and set all the files pertinent to her case on a wooden table abutting a rain-streaked picture window, beyond which our taxi-yellow rental car with bulbous fenders sat to its hubcaps in mud.

"It's cheery," I said.

"No, it isn't," she replied. She had changed into a brown Shetland wool sweater, put on wool socks, and was arranging her pens and legal pads on the grim veneer. "But the sky'll clear, you'll see, and then you'll thank me for bringing you to such an exquisite locale."

Both of us laughed at her attempt at an upper class British inflection. "Might you, dear Jack, take the chaise into town and fill the boot with victuals?"

I plucked the car key from her upturned palm. "Of course," I replied.

With only my learner's permit, I drove into Ambleside through fog and mist that hid everything beyond the white granite cairns bordering the road. As I did, I listened to commentators speaking French, then turned the radio knob to commentators speaking German. Though I knew only a little French and even less German, I imagined I was fluent in both, that I understood exactly the erudite points the commentators were making and whether I agreed with them or not. At the time I believed a native tongue one of the few definitive qualities a person could possess, but that like dying one's hair purple or joining the circus, even that was negotiable. Years had passed since I'd last sucked off Lucas Vite in the woods, and still I held out hope that he would return to me, that either he'd discover that he liked me better than his steady, Becca Pierce, a tenth grader whose precocious physical development rivaled his own, or that my Becca Pierce impression, upon which I'd labored like a method actor many nights before the bathroom mirror, squeezing my chest muscles between my arms to give the illusion of female breasts and my testicles between my legs to give the illusion of a vagina, would show up imperfections in the original.

By the time I parked the car in front of the cottage, my mother had lit a kerosene lamp, and her white hair glowed in the picture window. Drenched to the skin, I carried inside all the ingredients I would need for coq au vin. "How's your depression?" I asked.

A fifth of single malt shimmered caramel in the lantern light. She looked up from the legal pad on which she was scribbling. "The change of setting agrees with me, I must say," she said and took a sip from her tumbler. "How's yours?"

"Gone," I replied.

"Then our vacation has already accomplished everything I'd hoped."

But it hadn't accomplished anything. I'd lied, big whoop.

I'm looking at a postcard of Lake Windermere bought at the train depot the morning my mother and I departed for Heathrow. By now the postcard qualifies as an antique; the edges are crimped and the blank side has yellowed to the color of parchment. In italics at the bottom left corner is the copyright year, 1961, the last year the sun may have shone on that godforsaken region of a country I now visit twice a year on business and find perfectly charming. The photograph is of cobalt waves gilded in pink and gold against a backdrop of stone-faced mountains and cloudless sky, a scene so contrary to my memory of it I find it hard to believe I was ever there. What I remember is traversing miles of pasture on foot through fog that blanketed sheep braying all around me, a Frankenstein Monster without hope of ever achieving true intimacy with another human being, doomed to roving arctic ice floes.

In her defense, my mother could not have guessed that her armchair observation would be all the nourishment my nascent depression would need to blossom. As she delved ever deeper into her exculpation of a corporation blamed for marketing contraception that had resulted in cervical cancer in two out of three lab rats, I steeled myself for our dinners together, the London broil, leg of lamb, and shepherd's pie I prepared upon returning from my rain-soaked summer walks. Politics had been our default topic of conversation, but in England, Carter's race against Ford, who in pardoning Nixon had alienated much of the electorate, seemed more than an ocean away, and most nights we ate in silence punctuated by the pitter-patter of raindrops on the roof or, when the wind blew, rain spattering against the window.

On our last night in England my mother poured what remained of one fifth of Dalwhinnie into her tumbler and opened a second. "If you don't mind my asking, Jack, how often do you see your father?"

"That depends on what you mean by 'see,'" I replied. No one residing in Indian Hills could escape seeing him, zipping in his new persimmon Peugeot to one job site or another, often with a female companion in the passenger seat. Ever since Simone had returned to Quebec, a tidbit my mother had confided before Watergate gave us new, scintillating conversation with which to fill the dinner hour, my father seemed to take up with a different girlfriend every week.

"Do you talk to him?" she asked.

"Yawn," I replied.

"C'mon, Jack," she said. "Just because I want nothing to do with him doesn't mean you should."

"I'll never forgive how he treated you. All his unkind words."

"I was guilty of unkind words myself."

"But yours were true. Your assessment of him was spot on. And let's not forget, the judge sided with you."

"Your father loves you."

"He thinks I'm gay."

My mother picked at her mashed potatoes. Without taking a bite, she set her fork at the edge of her plate. "Aren't you?" she asked.

"Is Truman Capote a seven-foot point-guard for the New York Knicks? Does Liberace play the tuba? Has Andy Warhol just won Wimbledon?"

"It's okay if you are," she said.

"What part of 'I'm not gay' don't you understand?"

"It's your mannerisms, your particular affect, all quite lovely, don't get me wrong. But because of how you present yourself it hadn't occurred to me for a very long time that you might not be, you know, gay."

"Maybe Father was right," I said.

"About what?"

"Your being a castrating bitch."

My mother laughed in a way I hadn't heard since she was married. "So it's all my fault?"

"It isn't your fault. It's the alcohol. You drink like a fish and smell like a pig. What's worse, you don't make a lick of sense."

My mother could not have looked more aghast were I a vampire killer with my stake and hammer reared. "I'm sorry," she said.

"If this conversation is so important to you," I said, "strike it up when you're sober. You're no match for me when you're drunk."

"I suppose not," she said and, to her credit, never brought up the matter again.

Nights I dreamed of Hubert Humphrey. Sometimes we hunted pheasants, striding two abreast through waist-high cornstalks with our shotguns. Sometimes we trolled for walleyes, he with a sure hand on the throttle of a puttering outboard, I in the bow with my fishing rod extended over whitecaps. Once we barbecued baby back ribs on a backyard grill, both of us in chef's hats and checkered aprons. Never had I done any of these things, nor had I any desire to, yet I awoke from each in a bubble of warmth, as if the shared activity had provided a momentary reprieve from a life not yet worth living.

That summer lots in Indian Hills sold almost as quickly as they were subdivided, and in the afternoons, once I had tired of practicing my saxophone, I stared out my bedroom window at Lucas's house, more of which became visible hourly as lumber crews cleared elms with heavy machinery and hauled away limbs and brush. In the late afternoon when the last pickup had driven off, I hid behind bulldozers and backhoes abandoned for the night as Lucas and Becca bounced up and down on a trampoline. The Vites' home, too, had been built into the side of a hill, and as laughter sifted down into a valley where an embryonic cul-de-sac had taken root, I envisioned my father's houses blocking from view all but the Vites' rooftop patio where Lucas's parents, like my mother and I, lounged at twilight among potted geraniums and hanging fuchsia until mosquitoes drove them back indoors.

One evening when my mother was working late, I sprayed insect repellent over my arms, legs, face, and neck and crept over tire-rutted clods to the Vites' sliding glass door. I couldn't have said what motivated me, only that day by day I had been drawn through the horseshoe-shaped tracts of forestland and that afternoon had slipped unseen beneath the trampoline on which Lucas and Becca lay looking at cloud formations.

"There's Poseidon," Lucas said, "with his trident."

"And right behind him," Becca said, "Sally Fields as The Flying Nun."

"To me she looks like a World War II-era submarine," Lucas said.

"To me she looks like a loaf of bread," Becca said.

"Or a stuffed giraffe," Lucas said.

"Oh my god," Becca said, "I still have one of those."

"One of what?" Lucas asked.

"A stuffed giraffe."

Now on the other side of a sliding glass door, he reclined on a sofa facing me with his legs spread, Becca's sun-streaked hair draping his lap. As her head bobbed, her breasts expanded against his thighs like a horn-player's cheeks. But what could I do? Pound the glass? Scream to God to remove from Lucas's face the imbecilic grin? I had a princely image of him that shifted from the front of my brain to the back depending on the situation. Who was she to be so honored, so blessed? Had I not mastered control of my gag reflex and brought him to ever-mounting heights of pleasure, and not by slobbering all over him, but through carefully modulated contractions of the soft palate, pharynx, epiglottis, and tongue? How could I compete against someone whose lack of technique was accepted without protest?

I slapped a mosquito on my ear, and Lucas's eyes locked on the sliding glass door beyond which I lay like an angel cast into darkness. As he rose, Lucas's glistening erection hung suspended from his rippling torso, a staff so perfect I wondered that I had so much as grazed it with my lips. He pulled up his trousers, and as the door creaked on its runners, I squeezed my eyes closed and turned my face to the cement, praying every moment for a blow to the ribs or back of the head.

Through the dew-laden air Lucas's heat crested over me, spread-eagled in a block of light. Becca called to him, "What do you see?" and he replied, "Nothing," as the door creaked shut.

Three days later I met Gerald Ford—not *the* Gerald Ford, but a private contractor of the same name whose inexpensive, sloped-roof houses had won the approval of the subdivision's Building Commission in the wake of "seepage problems" in my father's flat-roofed homes. No one argued that my father's houses weren't sophisticated and chic, but for several years even my mother and I had had to place five-gallon plastic buckets about the dining room, living room, and bedrooms to catch drops from the lake under which we lived from late April to early June, when the runoff from five feet of snow finally evaporated. If every summer she had our roof resealed, every spring she awoke under a damp eiderdown, or slipped on the parquet, or set her legal brief in a puddle on the coffee table. Once I asked her why she was crying and she said she wasn't, just as a teardrop separated from the ceiling and landed on her cheek. If by then we'd resigned ourselves to the problem, several of our neighbors had not. No fewer than five plaintiffs were suing my father to the tune of six million dollars for "structural erosion" due to "avoidable flaws in construction."

"Your father's homes belong on the French Riviera," she said, a Szechuan shrimp to celebrate the third anniversary of her divorce held aloft by chopsticks, "and these people purchased theirs knowing full well they were making impractical decisions. This isn't Provence, it's Minnesota, and now they want your father to pay for their flights of fancy. *Please*."

"He could sure use your help now, couldn't he?"

She sighed. "I'd offer to represent him if I thought

for a second it wouldn't be construed as a conflict of interest."

"Would it be a conflict of interest?" I asked.

"I don't know."

Her admission of allegiance to my father gave me pause. I'd thought of us as allied against a common enemy. Still, my father's problems were the least of my worries as I wandered Iroquois Trail's winding terraces on a lazy afternoon in late July. Even when he pulled up beside me in his Peugeot and smiled from the driver's seat as if to say, *I am at fault, I ask for your forgiveness, I love and accept you exactly as you are*, and called out, "Jack, don't walk away. I'll take off the rest of the afternoon. We'll go see a Twins' game. They're playing the A's," I was speculating about the start of the school year and on whether Lucas's having caught me spying on him and Becca would have any negative consequences.

I replied in my faggiest voice, "I'm afraid I must decline," and off he drove.

If I knew Lucas, and I believed I did, he wouldn't want what I had on him leaked to the public. But as my father sped away it occurred to me I had nothing to lose and possibly everything to gain by spreading rumors about Lucas and me. Kids already whispered "homo," "fairy," "pansy," "queer," "queen," and "fruit" to one another in the halls and cafeteria whenever I passed. Were a well-meaning classmate to confront me about Lucas, I could plead the Fifth and kindergartners would be wagging their heads on the playground, asking one another what the world had come to.

Lucas was our class's golden child, the ideal to which

every boy aspired and for which every girl longed, the JV quarterback to whom the Varsity coach had already pinned hopes of winning back-to-back state championships, the athlete whose academic shortcomings teachers overlooked as long as his afternoon performances invited comparisons to Namath, Staubach, Tarkington, and Starr. That Lucas himself had begun to believe in his gilt-edged future as evidenced by his cloying façade of self-deprecating politeness. But I knew what others didn't, that he'd once taken great pleasure in beating me up. It was from these beatings, after all, that our romance had sprung. If I insinuated to one and all that I was his true love, perhaps I could provoke the sleeping bully in him again.

Indeed, I was fantasizing about receiving an upper cut to the mouth followed by a jab to the jaw, after which Lucas would kiss my bleeding lips, when I next saw Hubert Humphrey, standing before his mailbox sorting his mail.

"Senator Humphrey!" I yelled, running toward him. "Senator Humphrey! It's me! Jack Reville!"

Had Hubert Humphrey worn a hearing aid? "Senator Humphrey!" I yelled again, by then mere feet from him, and as he lurched as if from an attack dog, mail fluttered from his hands into foliage bordering the lane.

"Allow me," I said, plunging my fingers into ivy for a *Sports Illustrated*, phone bill, and grocery store circular, only recognizing it as the poison variety when leaves tickled my forearms.

I handed him his mail, and he regarded me from

the other side of his mailbox.

"What did you call me?"

Up close, his resemblance to Hubert Humphrey was fleeting at best. "I thought you were Senator Humphrey," I said.

"Really?" He wagged his boulder of a head. "Well, I'm not him, though I share a name with our current president. Now how funny is that? Not very if you're the less famous of us. When the president vetoes a bill, no one thinks of their contractor." Gerald Ford sighed and chuckled. "This is the first time I've ever been mistaken for someone who *lost* a bid for the White House. And you know what? I'm guessing it won't be the last."

He nodded at a campaign poster for Carter planted across the street at the bottom of a neighbor's drive. Indian Hills was littered with them, which corroborated the change in popular sentiment Hubert Humphrey had predicted at the airport.

"I hope you don't mind my asking," Gerald Ford said, "but I couldn't help noticing something about you—"

"What?" I said, irritated by anyone with a theory about me.

"Ah, it's nothing." He hung his head and turned to the white pickup idling at the entrance to his own wooded drive. On the driver's side door was printed

GERALD FORD CONSTRUCTION
OMAHA, NEBRASKA

"Wait," I said.

In profile he could've been Hubert Humphrey, but when he faced me the illusion was ruined, the wrinkles surrounding his eyes and mouth unused to mirth, his sallow cheeks and jowls leaden, inanimate. In his black poplin jacket and white button-down open at the collar, he might've passed for a down-on-his-luck lounge singer, were his actual profession not betrayed by the crusts of mud on his blue patent leather buckle-ups.

"Go ahead. Ask me whatever you were going to."

"Like I said, it's no business of mine and Lord knows I make a point of keeping my nose out of other people's affairs, but when you mistook me for Hubert Humphrey just now, it sounded to me like you actually knew him. Is Hubert Humphrey a friend of yours?"

"He's more than a friend," I said, swelling with pride at having been recognized by the Senator three years after meeting him. "He's like a second father to me."

"Like a second father, huh?" A cockeyed smile rose to Gerald Ford's face. "One question always begs another, doesn't it? It's why I don't ask many."

"What else do you want to know?" I asked.

"That's right," he said. "Put old Gerald on the spot. Make him squirm a little. Turn the tables. What I want to know, now that you've put the screws to old Gerald, is what's up with your first father if the venerable Hubert Humphrey is your second."

"We don't get along," I said. "Never have, never will."

Gerald pinched the bridge of his nose as if staving off a headache. "Say no more, say no more. Your entire story has come to me in a vision. I'd say what you need right now is a bratwurst with all the trimmings. You eaten lunch?"

I wagged my head.

"Then get in the truck, laddy. Old Gerald may not be cordon bleu, but he's not bad with a pair of tongs."

He removed a pile of blueprints from the passenger seat, and I sat down in a cab that smelled of fresh cologne and cigarettes. "I should apologize for the mess," he said, "but I won't. Like questions, apologies are habit-forming and lead to untenable situations over time." He set the blueprints on my lap.

"Are you married?" I asked.

"Three times," he replied.

"I'm sorry," I said.

"Don't be.

In the woods on either side of his drive construction crews laid foundations for homes accessible by streets graded but not yet paved. When we pulled up to his house, I told Gerald that it was one my father had built, and he sank into his seat as if concrete were being poured through a siphon into an opening where his head rested precariously on a triple chin.

"So you're Jack Reville's boy," he said at last. "You go by Jack, too?"

I nodded.

"Well, one thing's for certain, Jack. Your father builds a pretty home. Yep, when I moved into this one three months ago, I said to myself, 'Gerald, this is just the sort of luxury home you'd be building if you'd studied architecture like you were going to. But no, fresh out of high school you had to go work for your uncle and learn homebuilding from the ground up, by actually building them. But c'est la vie. At least a dumb ass like me gets to live in one, which is more than any of my ex-wives can say.' Come on, Jack, I bet you're starved."

I wasn't, but Gerald Ford had appeared as if in answer to a question I didn't know how to ask.

"Uh-huh," he said as he unlocked the front door, "your father's homes are real treats for the eyes." His entryway, like ours, opened into undifferentiated space. Free of dividing walls, the living room, dining room, and kitchen flowed one into the other. I sat at a barstool at his kitchen island, the same as I did at home, as he contemplated the contents of his splayed refrigerator-freezer. "But I'm going to let you in on a little secret, Jack. In twenty years, every one of your father's homes will have been torn down and in its place will stand one of my mine."

He set a plate containing six uncooked sausages on the kitchen counter. "Now you can either have one of these or one of these."

"One of what?" I asked, which was when I saw that he was exposing himself to me.

I knew what I wanted, and as I knelt before Gerald, he said, "There's a good boy."

The long and short of it is, Molly wants a divorce. She says that for nearly twenty years she and I have lived a lie and that practicing her newfound "art" has brought her to an "epiphany": namely, that "role-play" has no place in a marriage of "kindred spirits." Forced by circumstance into the *role* of epistemologist, I have argued that spirits cannot express themselves except through approximations of meaning and that the limitations imposed on them by language and the corporeal bodies in which they're housed lace every intimation with at least a degree of deceit. But this isn't a tenet Molly wishes to entertain, for she has found a "soul mate" in one of her teachers, a massage therapist and guru in his sixties named Ferenc, to whom, I'm given to understand, she is "able to say anything and everything and be perfectly understood" despite his frequent mellifluous lapses into Hungarian, which Molly is acquiring with the help of Berlitz tapes.

We haven't told our sons, but I suspect they'll take the news with their chins up, and perhaps even be relieved that their family will soon resemble those of many of their friends. Ray, our youngest, is the more self-conscious, always fretting over appearances and fearful at Sunday services that we look as if we've stepped from a time capsule launched in 1955. And it isn't because Molly and I have a penchant for vintage clothing. It's because we worship as a nuclear unit, seated in our pew from tallest to shortest, which among Methodists is a vanishing phenomenon as far as I can tell. This memoir hasn't been easy to write, and as I embark upon the most haunting installment of all, I can hear my sons chopping carrots and celery for their mother in the kitchen. I adore my wife, and while I don't expect anyone but my mother to shed a tear over the loss my sons and I will suffer if she leaves me, I'm weeping as I write, devastated at the thought of no longer hearing the little song Molly hums before falling asleep at night, a cross between "How Deep is the Ocean" and "My Funny Valentine," sipping kir royales on a summer evening, solving the Sunday crossword, hunting for antiques, playing bridge, griping about work. The list, which includes frequent lovemaking, goes on and on.

Of course, I take exception to Molly's claim that our relationship is based on a lie. Not many days after she told me she wanted a divorce, I told her the story of meeting Hubert Humphrey not once but twice as a kid and admitted to her that my first real love affair had been with a man more than thirty years my senior who resembled him. I told her about my homosexual awakening at age twelve and my refusal to speak openly about it with anyone, even Gerald, with whom I maintained a covert relationship for over two years, amazing since it began with a poison ivy rash that linked us as lovers. Long story short, without Gerald's understanding and guidance, I'm not sure I would have "lived to tell the tale," for as often as I may have joked about my depression in earlier pages of this manuscript, I was suicidal before I met him and afterward I no longer entertained fantasies of dying at the fists and boots of Lucas Vite. Though some will say that I was merely the victim of a sexual predator—and indeed this story would be incomplete if I failed to mention that for more than a decade Gerald's name has appeared on state and national child molester registers—I bristle at the thought. As much a parent as a boyfriend, he saw me through many difficulties, not the least of which was learning that my father had disappeared, then six months later that he had died of liver failure on the streets of Quebec, pleading with Simone to take him back, which she refused to do, though he was bleeding from the eyes.

I told Molly all this, then asked whether any of it had come as a shock to her. "No," she said.

"What if I'd told you all this twenty years ago," I said, "before we married?"

"Frankly, none of it would've surprised me then either," she replied.

"Then where is the lie?" I asked. "In my liking to enter you from behind? In my thinking you look better with your hair cut short?"

A neighbor had taken our sons to a Diamondbacks game. Molly and I rested on chaise lounges on our deck overlooking the seventeenth green as a man and woman in their seventies wearing matching Izod golf shirts replaced the pin. Between Molly and me sat a half-eaten smoked trout with its head still on, a basket of water crackers, a third of a bottle of chardonnay. I refilled Molly's glass.

"Just because a lie is out in the open doesn't make it any less of one," she said.

In the kitchen Ray and Leo call me to supper, after which we'll play "The Pink Panther Theme," they on the drums and electric bass and me on the tenor sax, Molly swooning like a teenager on our living room couch as if tonight were the same as any other. Perhaps it will be. And tomorrow night, too. And years from now when our sons are married and have children of their own,

Molly and I will look up from a game of Scrabble and laugh. Stranger things have happened.

Today not one of my father's homes remains. Perhaps if one did I would make a pilgrimage to it. The last time I saw him was from Gerald's driveway. October, the trees had shed their foliage, and in response to an argument Gerald and I had been having about public displays of affection, I fled from his breakfast nook onto asphalt silver with frost in nothing but a terrycloth robe and red Dacron thong he'd given me on Valentine's Day. Not amused, Gerald stood on the stoop in his pinstriped pajamas as I performed a striptease, prodding him the while to hold me, kiss me, save me from myself. He could have me any way he wished, I said, if only he would demonstrate his love for me, and demonstrate he did as my father, in plain view on the second story of a house he would never finish, looked on.

High Art and Low

The Witnesses, a mother-daughter team, disliked her because she was Catholic and prayed to the Virgin and other idols, and when they arrived at the door to check on her sister Sam, pass along the latest edition of *The Watchtower*, and repeat God's promise to the faithful, Tabitha fled to her parents' bedroom. On the vanity rested their urns—the pink marble housed her mother's ashes, the yellow her dad's—and as Sam and the women chatted in the living room about the massage therapist who'd been arrested a few days before for lacing a female client's Dr. Pepper with GHB and molesting her on his table while she dozed, Tabitha said a novena for her little sister.

"O Most Blessed Mother, heart of love, heart of mercy, ever listening, caring, consoling, hear our prayer."

One thing was certain, their mother hadn't done Sam any favors during the final decade of her life. Bedridden for most of it, she'd relied on Sam for practically everything, from Epsom Salts baths and meals cooked to order to books on demonic possession, read aloud to pass the hours between lunch and supper, supper and dawn. During her brief remissions and between her treatments, their mother had brought Sam with her on specimen-collecting expeditions to the vacant lots of their subdivision, scaring up rattlers, copperheads, scorpions, and other vermin for the decorative coasters, plaques, and whatnot she made in the kitchen, sit-

49

uating in molds creatures she'd frozen in the Frigidair, then pouring molten polyurethane over them. When they had cooled, she loaded them into the Buick and sold them on consignment at the truck stops and strip clubs along the interstate from Weatherford to Mingus and Highway 51 north to Decatur.

Two years after their mother's death, a few of her horrid objets d'art could evidently still be found inside Wet Willies, a topless joint on the service road not far from the house, near the entrance booth on card tables displaying two-for-one porn videos, taxidermy, and other vile bric-a-brac. Before such colossal grossness they'd stood as girls, a 12-year-old Tabitha aghast as her 10-year-old sister paged through a dog-eared comic book featuring on the cover a three-breasted female alien or, worse, fingered a battery-operated vagina free of its torn box. All the while their mother haggled with the owner, William Sweet, for more sales space.

Sweet William, as he was affectionately known, sat in a wheelchair behind a sheet of Plexiglas perforated at the level of his mustache-draped lips like a telephone receiver's mouthpiece, sipping a boilermaker no matter the hour, his iron-colored hair a lean-to beneath which the sunken eyes of God peered out. "Don't you think the merchandise a little mature for them girls of yours?" he'd said on more than one of their visits.

"They'll see worse and they'll see better, and at least know the difference between high art and low," their mother replied.

"OK, Lydia, you can move a possum or two to make room for your knickknacks."

"Girls, you heard Sweet William."

Now Sam worked there, cocktail waitressing or so she said.

In the living room, she offered the Witnesses iced mint tea she'd steeped in a Saran-wrapped pitcher on the front porch. "You must be parched," Tabitha heard her say, "what with all the walking door-to-door."

"As your children," Tabitha said, "we implore your intercession with Jesus your Son. Please receive with understanding and compassion the petitions we place before you, especially regarding Sam, who sacrificed much and suffered greatly during our mother's illness and untimely death from endometrial cancer and whose father, as you know, was also taken from us prematurely a year ago in a small airplane crash."

Through the walls of paneled sheetrock even whispers carried. In Texas, it was impolite to accept anything without twice declining, and sure enough, Sam's third offer was the charm. The springs of the davenport squeaked as the women made themselves comfortable. Tabitha had spied them through the peephole upon their arrival feathering their orange pageboys with wide, pale fingers. Who, she wanted to know, invited Witnesses into their homes? In Denton, she'd once dated a musicologist who'd delighted in debating proselytizers, quoting scripture and attacking doctrine with a vigor that made her wonder if he believed exegesis a key to getting laid. But even he had kept a screen door between himself and the apostles as if fearful of contracting, at the very least, an unpleasant skin condition. Here Sam knew the mother and daughter by name—they were Kay and Ginny—where they worked—at Ridgmar Travel and the Wendy's in Linwood—and even the Kingdom Hall at which they worshipped—the one on James Avenue off of I-20.

"So what you're saying," Sam said, "if I get your drift, is that poor woman getting drugged unconscious and felt up by that dirty bird in Richland Hills is a sign of the end times?"

"We grant you that as a single incident," said the mother, Kay, "it may not seem like much. But in the context of everything else that's happening locally and globally, it's easy to see that it's part of a pattern. Do you read the newspaper?"

"I watch CNN," Sam replied.

"Well, I don't recommend the news at all, not in any form," said Kay, "except as a means of keeping abreast of Satan's handiwork. Do you believe in Satan?"

"Of course," Sam said. "A girl's gotta have something to blame her evilness on."

"So you believe Satan a laughing matter?" the daughter Ginny asked.

"No," Sam said. "I believe Satan was cast from heaven for wanting to trade places with the Almighty and since the dawn of creation has recruited the souls of the damned for a final showdown."

"At least you believe in Armageddon," said Kay. "Many of the lost don't. They believe Satan doesn't exist. But when we look in their eyes, we see him grinning back at us in the darkness of their pupils." She emitted a plaintive sigh, and even it carried. "Of course, Ginny and I will speak to them for as long as they'll have us, but in a real sense the battles for their souls have been lost. Haven't they, Ginny?"

"Yes," Ginny agreed. "But the Bible does make clear that there won't be room in paradise for everyone."

"True," said Kay. "*Revelations*, Chapter Fourteen, Verse Three. 'And no man could learn that song but the hundred and forty-four thousand, which were redeemed from the earth.'"

"Dear Jesus," Tabitha said, rosary beads entwined about her fingers like a serpent.

Though it meant missing rehearsals of *Giselle*, she'd driven down from Denton for a week to help her sister through the painful anniversaries of their parents' deaths. Two years ago from the previous Saturday, their mother had sat up abruptly in the bed she and Sam were sharing, hissed, "No," as if in answer to Sam's prayers for her recovery, and passed away just as daybreak filtered through the blinds. Then, exactly a year and one week later, in the twin-engine Rebel their father had built in the garage from parts he'd ordered from catalogs, he handed over the controls to a flight student who, having never landed a plane before, piloted it into power lines that flipped it nose under tail onto the runway where it exploded into flames, killing them both.

You couldn't make shit like this up, Tabitha had told her housemates in Denton, all graduates of the University of North Texas who'd been unable to do anything with their degrees in the tanking economy and, like her, had scraped by for almost a decade as temps, baristas, substitutes, and clerks by day, artists, writers, dancers, and musicians by night. Only Winslow, nearly twenty years older than the rest of them and still in school, had lost his father. The rest still had both parents and thought losing a mother and father within fifty-three weeks of each other unsettling at best. Was it mere coincidence? Part of some divine plan? A curse? What she hadn't the heart to tell any of them, though, not even Winslow, was that the flight student whose charred remains were uncovered from the wreckage had been a practicing Shiite Muslim from Qatar named Arhum Hussein, a respected petrophysicist a few years older than she who drove up from Houston on the weekends for flying instruction and once, while she was at home visiting her dad and Sam, had even asked her on a date.

Why so many of her father's flight students had been of Arab descent, she didn't know, but while the flight school's demographic was often a subject of derision among the other pilots, her father had refused to participate in such talk, happy to be in the company of anyone interested in horizontal situations and vertical speeds, course deviations and decision heights, regardless of race or creed. Whether he'd been right or wrong to be so trusting, with his death went any semblance of family normalcy, and she didn't want his memory sullied by crass racist jokes about pilots-in-training-of-a-certain-ethnicity having no interest in learning to land, only to fly. She'd heard the jokes for the better part of her adult life, heard them even at her father's memorial service, and didn't need to hear them from college friends who'd literally been in college on 9/11.

"Your mother," said Kay, "was clearly among the enlightened."

"She was?" said Sam.

"Most certainly," said Kay. "Indeed, I wouldn't be surprised to learn Jehovah Himself had appeared to her in a vision."

"If He did," said Sam, "she never mentioned it."

"It may have happened when she was very young," said Ginny, "but with no one to interpret the experience for her, she never learned what it meant."

"Mother wasn't what anyone would call 'spiritual,'" said Sam. "She called religion 'opium for the massa.'"

"'Opium for the massa'?" asked Kay. That Sam was the queen of malapropisms would have been amusing except that every one that fell from her lips made Tabitha cringe. Sam wasn't touched, though someone could be forgiven for thinking so. She'd just never advanced beyond eleventh grade. Their mother's ill health had seen to it.

"Well, as my daughter said, your mother may not have known what the vision meant or even remembered it in adulthood. But look here, Sam. What's this?"

"A paperweight?"

"Yes, but what's inside it?" asked Ginny. "Preserved in plastic?"

"Just some scorpion Mother found on the driveway."

"And that?" asked Kay.

"Just some tarantula crossing the street when Mother was leaving the beauty salon."

"And that?" asked Ginny.

"That there," said Sam, "is a baby diamondback rattler Mother smoked out from its underground lair with an M-80 firecracker."

"And that?" asked Kay.

"A baby copperhead. You can see its mother over at the After Five. Johnny Pennyacre's got her hanging over a booth, says it's a real conversation piece, especially popular with out-of-towners."

"Your mother," said Kay, "whether she knew it or not, was realizing a vision of God's promise to the faithful."

It was then that Tabitha stepped from the shadows of the hallway, her patience tried long enough. "Out," she said, the silver crucifix at the end of her string of rose petal beads before her like a talisman. She pointed it first at Kay, then at Ginny. "Out, I said."

The work she still had to do with her sister, a shut-in for most of her life and beyond gullible, would be hard enough without the Witnesses filling her head with nonsense. Their mother had been many things, but an instrument of God she wasn't. She'd been a tyrant, a megalomaniac, and an adulteress, and, were there any validity to what Sam had been telling her when the door chimes announced the arrival of their unwanted guests, a sexual deviant if not a child molester.

"Oh," said Kay, as undeterred by Tabitha's intrusion as she might be by a client needing rerouting. "Ginny and I were just commenting on your mother's artworks. We believe her a visionary, and that filling your home with creatures was her way of preparing for the

Earth's return to Eden."

"If you think so," Tabitha said, "you're welcome to them. Take as many as you like." From the wall socket she unplugged a table lamp, in the clear plastic base of which a coral snake lay on pebbles as if sunning itself. When she had set the thing on Kay's lap, she gave to Ginny a black widow spider at the bottom of a shot glass. The junk their mother had made in her lifetime, from coffee table tops to coasters and ashtrays, could fill a pickup bed.

"No one, and I mean no one," said Tabitha, "who knew our mother ever mistook her for a visionary. Most thought she was a witch. They were scared of her and rightly so."

Kay and Ginny, in matching burnt umber skirts and blazers, turned to each other and rose from the couch, their orange pageboys as pendulous as mace blades above their padded shoulders. "We can take a hint," Kay said, "and if you don't mind, we'll leave these with you," and she and Ginny placed the gifts Tabitha had given them on the sofa cushions. "They don't quite fit our décor."

Ginny reminded Sam to peruse the literature she and her mother had brought to the house and to join them at the Kingdom Hall at her earliest convenience. "You know where it's located," she said. "It's no more than a twenty minute drive from here. You may bring your sister if you wish."

"We've saved harder cases," Kay said.

"Just don't wait forever," Ginny said. "You don't *have* forever." And with that Tabitha closed the door on the ladies' well-appointed, if penumbral, backsides.

In the living room Sam rocked in their father's La-Z-Boy with her arms wrapped around her knees, her bare feet on the claret-colored cloth. "I swear you've gotten ruder than Mother. Kay and Ginny meant no harm, and you treated them like leopards."

"Lepers?" said Tabitha as she sat down where the Witnesses had been, her own bare feet on the coffee table less than an inch from a rattler's forked tongue, the puddles beneath the ladies' half-finished iced teas magnifying its small, yellow eye.

"Whatever," Sam replied.

Tabitha had counted on pissing her off when she'd first decided to show Kay and Ginny the literal hell awaiting them beyond the reach of A/C. In khaki shorts and one of their father's work shirts with American Legend and his name, Joe, stitched above the breast pocket, Sam looked every bit the teenager she still was emotionally, psychologically, even physically, her complexion unlined and unblemished, her blond, shoulder-length hair, which had never had anything more astringent applied to it than baby shampoo rinsed with well water, showing no hint of gray. Evilest of all, Sam had inherited their mother's metabolism, so at twenty-nine she weighed 103 pounds, the same as she had in high school, though she ate what she pleased, little of it healthy.

"Tell me I didn't hear you say, 'Opium for the massa,'" Tabitha said.

Sam pressed the power button on the remote control, directed it at the flat screen, and on it came a shark devouring a seal in a garish display of teeth, blood, and vain anguish. "You know as well as I it's what Mother called religion."

"She called it 'the opiate of the masses,'" Tabitha replied. "Masses. As in, teeming. She was quoting Marx." Tabitha laughed. "What, was Mother auditioning for a role in *Roots*? 'Don't go to church, massa. It's bad for you, massa. Smoke this, massa. It'll save your soul, massa.'"

Then Sam was laughing, too, her pissy-ness nothing more than an infant needing coaxing back to sleep. The thought of their white, skinny-assed mother cast as a 19th century African slave was funny, after all.

"Can't you just see Mother," Sam said, "being whipped in the shed?" She snorted. "'No, massa. No, massa. No, massa.'"

"So tell me again," said Tabitha, wiping her eyes, "just what she made you do back when she was sick and you and she were sleeping in the same bed." It's what they had been talking about before The Witnesses arrived.

"She didn't *make* me do anything," Sam replied and returned her attention to the TV.

"You said you touched her down there," Tabitha said. "What did you mean by 'down there'?"

"Her cooch," Sam said. "Her vajayjay. I touched her vajayjay. There, happy?"

"You touched her vagina?" said Tabitha. "You masturbated her?"

"If you want to get all clinician about it," Sam said.

"Dear Lord," said Tabitha.

During her decade away, she'd feared things at home had taken a dark turn, felt so guilty about it she'd turned to Catholicism for the solace of knowing that nothing was foreign, however awful, to God or his intermediaries and that He and they were always available to those in need. When first told of her plans to convert, her housemates had thought devoting a year of Tuesday nights to RCIA a great waste of time for a classically trained ballerina and choreographer with a forty-hour-a-week day job as a cashier at a savings and loan, but as the date of her baptism approached their respect for her grew. They admired the perfumed luminosity of her bedroom, the silver crosses that shimmered through her necklines of black lace, the new bearing she'd acquired upon learning from Deacon Gottlieb that the Virgin had her back. And why wouldn't they? She partied just as hard as she always had, bedded whomever she pleased, but now with the faith that through divinity all sins were forgiven and the spirit cleansed. As she rose smiling from her full immersion in the sanctuary of Immaculate Conception, they applauded from a front pew, and afterward celebrating at the Abbey, a bereted Winslow sipped from his pint of La Fin Du Monde and said, "I swear, only Tabitha could make Catholicism seem cool." The others agreed.

"To Tabitha, patron saint of what?"

"Seamstresses," Tabitha replied, then told them the story of her namesake's resurrection in answer to the fervent prayers of the Apostle Peter.

"Mother was in such pain," Sam said. "You have no

idea. Nothing else gave her any pleasure."

"Really?"

"And she was on a lot of morphine, if that makes any difference."

"Maybe it does, maybe it doesn't," Tabitha said. "Who knows?" The air conditioner hummed, and she wondered if Sam had changed the filter, if she even knew to do that at three-month intervals. If her prayer for the resurrection of her parents were answered and they were to burst from their urns, by God she'd give them an earful.

"Where was Dad when all of this was going on?" she asked.

"Where do you think he was?" Sam replied. "Asleep in your old bedroom. He never heard a thing. Honest."

"Unbelievable," Tabitha said.

"Do you think I shouldn't have done what I did?" Sam asked. "Do you think it was sinful? That I'm sinful?"

"I'm in no position to say," Tabitha replied.

"You weren't there," said Sam.

"You're right," Tabitha said. "I wasn't."

"It's like with Dad," said Sam. "Should he have given the controls to Arhum?"

"No," said Tabitha, "it's nothing like that."

Sam turned off the television. "Well, I'm going to Sonic. Then I'm going over to Wet Willies to see about a shift."

"Cocktail waitressing?" Tabitha asked.

"What do you think?" Sam replied.

"You're stripping, aren't you?" Tabitha said. "It's

61

come to that, hasn't it? And people know it, too. You think they don't? You think they don't see Mother's Buick parked in front of that claptrap from I-20 and know exactly what you and your squirrelly ass are up to?"

"I don't park in the front," Sam replied, "I park in the back. And anyway, I don't care what anyone knows or *thinks* they know. When I'm there it feels like home. And I'm good at it, too. I'm really good. You want me to show you, Tabby?"

No, Tabitha thought as her sister unbuttoned their father's shirt. Tabitha closed her eyes as from the speakers came "Who Let the Dogs Out?" When she opened them, Sam stood before her topless, her nipples beige in the shuttered light, her expression one of studied grace. "It all happens behind glass. I can't see anyone."

She spun on the carpet. "That's a fouetté," Tabitha said.

"What's a fouetté?" Sam asked.

"A spin," Tabitha said. "I'll show you."

She rose from the couch and assumed an effacé devant, the working leg pointed, one arm extended and the other arced. She could blame her parents or she could blame herself. Who was she, or they, to believe anyone could parent her sister? Or maybe she could try to see them all, herself included, as God did, through rising smoke, drawing a pipe to His lips.

Red Cinquefoil

I was playing the nickel slots, three at a time, at an Indian casino off I-40 twenty minutes west of Albuquerque when the first wheel of Wild Wilderness locked on canned beans, the second did the same, and the third teased the pay line between canned beans and campfire logs. Though not a man of strong religious convictions, on a whim I prayed to Saint Anthony. I asked him to gently guide the machine to its maximum payoff and help me reclaim a small portion of the large sum I'd lost to a gambling addiction with which, on a Friday when my youngest daughter Cecily expected me for dinner at six, I'd struggled for more than fifty years. I told Saint Anthony that, if he existed and weren't too busy helping other, more deserving souls to lend me a hand, I'd rectify my profligate ways, walk a narrower path, and with my winnings effect change that would honor the glory of his master and mine. I admitted I was a weak but far from humble vessel who was susceptible to vices of many varieties, and that for these and other failings I hadn't been the clean instrument for magnanimous acts God, if He existed, had no doubt hoped for when He created me, and just as I was about to list the changes I, at seventy-one, was prepared to make on His—which is to say, if He were inclined, in His most holy of hearts, to care, even an ounce—behalf, the slot machine lit up from within and began to quake.

Myriad bulbs hidden beneath a casing of slick polyurethane unfurled in rippling banners of cherry, apricot, and blue. Flugelhorns, a battalion, performed "Save the Last Dance for Me" as fireworks exploded in the background. More lights, located deep within the contraption, flickered like stars, like distant galaxies, as teapots whistled, chainsaws whirred, and a laugh track stopped and started. A crowd of gamblers gathered around me, slapped my shoulder, patted my back. A woman removed an oxygen mask from her face, took a puff of her Marlboro, and cried, "You've won!" Balanced atop her wheeled cylinder was an ashtray overflowing with butts, into which she tapped the end of her cigarette and pointed at the payoff screen where animated woodchucks played leapfrog over a jackpot of $1,597,244.10. "You're a millionaire, laddy," exclaimed a man in his fifties wearing a tartan kilt, carrying Uileann pipes, and supporting himself on prosthetic legs. To the cacophony he added a Scottish rendition of "Adios, mi Corazon" as from the slot machine, but sounding as if at the mic in the casino lounge, Bobby Darin crooned "Splish Splash."

A skinny blond wisp-of-a-thing, no older than twenty-five, removed one of a dozen strings of mardi gras beads from around her neck. She motioned for me to lower my head and as she draped a necklace over my ears she shouted, "Will you marry me, grandpa?" I shouted back, "Show me your intended." I assumed she'd meant for me to conduct her ceremony—in seventy-one years stranger things had been asked of me—and she directed a lazy finger at the white hairs tufting

like a dickey from the collar of my favorite lucky Hawaiian short-sleeve.

I sipped my Jack and Coke. I'd been divorced since
'75, the year my then-wife Annabel was treated for
syphilis she'd contracted from me. Back then we lived
with our daughters, Cecily and Kate, then five and sev-
en, in a trailer at the southern-most edge of the Nevada
Test Site. Four days a week I oversaw crews of min-
ers and roughnecks whose job it was to plant nuclear
devices, "pits" we called them, hundreds if not thousands of feet beneath the surface of the desert. Fridays
I reported to the Department of Energy's offices in Las
Vegas where briefings never lasted longer than an hour
and afternoons were mine. I didn't blame Annabel. In
her position I would have left me, too, always promis-
ing to steer clear of the casinos, cut back on my drinking, quit smoking, and end my affairs with particular
prostitutes to whom I'd grown attached.

"You wouldn't be pulling my leg, would you?" I
asked the girl, imagining how pretty my living room
would look with her in it. Since '94, the year Bill Clin-
ton killed the nuclear weapons testing program, I'd
lived by myself in a west Vegas subdivision. I'd been
given the choice of a desk job with the D. of E. or early retirement with full benefits. I considered telling
them to shove their paper-sorting where the sun didn't
shine, but if you'd spent thirty years planting nukes in
the earth you'd know there isn't such a place and I quietly retired.

"No," she replied.

"Okay," I said. "You're on. Let's get married."

I reached into a pocket of my Bermuda shorts and handed her a piece of sludge, glass formed when the first pit I'd ever planted, codenamed "Red Cinquefoil," was detonated and underneath the desert temperatures in excess of a 100 million degrees Centigrade opened a cavity roughly the size of the town we lived in, Indian Springs, and ensconced it in melted rock that grew opaque and shiny as it cooled. Trapped in the piece I'd given the girl were tiny air bubbles commemorating the moment of the blast. "We'll use that until we find us a proper engagement ring," I said. The last I'd checked, it was radiating between 40 and 45 milliroentgen an hour, less radiation than one might receive during a visit to the dentist or, back when Annabel and I bought our oldest Kate her first pair of patent leather sandals, a trip to the shoe store.

As my intended examined what was undoubtedly the oddest "rock" she'd ever seen, I said above the ruckus, "If you're a gold digger, darling, it's only fair to warn you. The odds of my dying anytime soon aren't good."

She looked at me with wet blue eyes. "Why would I want you to die?"

"For the money?" I glanced again at the payoff screen where my 1.5 million and change pulsated like Joey Bishop's name on a '70's Caesar's Palace marquee.

"I'm not marrying you for money," she said with a pout. "I'm marrying you for luck."

"Got plenty of that," I said, "both good and bad."

"It seems pretty good to me right now," she said. "You're the first jackpot winner I've seen since I got here."

"When was that, sweetheart?"

"Tuesday."

Already I was imagining Cecily and her husband Mike's reaction to this Kansas blond waif-of-a-girl stepping out of my Lincoln in her men's white V-neck t-shirt belted at the waist. Two weeks before, my youngest daughter had given birth to Mike Jr., whom I was ostensibly on my way to meet. Though the occasion was joyous and my trunk filled with sacks of baby clothes, some of which Cecily herself had worn, I wouldn't be telling the complete story if I didn't also confess an ulterior motive: a year earlier my daughters' stepfather, J.R., had died of colon cancer in Denver, and while I would never wish anything as evil as that on another human being, now that J.R. was dead I could take pleasure, especially in the company of those who had known him, in having outlived an ophthalmologist who, according to my daughters, had abstained from alcohol, tobacco, and prescription drugs; who exercised obsessively and ate farm-raised salmon and trout three times a week; and who regularly faulted me, in the presence of my daughters, for exposing them as children to radiation that, he said, would give them cancer later in their lives.

Now if Cecily, Kate, or Annabel, God forbid, contracted cancer, it wouldn't be because of the environmental doses to which I'd exposed them; no, there was a reason 51% of the roughly 120,000 men who'd worked at the Nevada Test Site between '62 and '92 were still alive, some of them in their nineties: radiation at the levels we and our families had experienced

67

was beneficial to human life. And all of us had known it. It was why we brought sludge home with us from the Site, why we set it alongside geodes on our mantels and bookshelves and carried it in our pockets like rabbits' feet.

"Tell me your name, darling," I said.

"Tell me yours first," the girl replied.

"Gordon Langley," I said.

"Gordon Langley, God bless you. This is for you."

Then my angel wrapped her arms around me, drew my lips to hers, and our tongues danced a tango in the ballroom of our mouths. In a periphery blurred by her wheat blond hair, two Indians in dark suits and one wearing a turquoise calf-length dress pressed through the throng. A photographer and a uniformed policeman followed in their wake. In no time they had formed a celebratory crescent around us, but they could wait. I was a lover and in no hurry for our kiss to end, so enveloped was I by my new young lover's scent, the taste of her saliva, the softness of her breasts against my chest.

When at last we separated, I unzipped my fanny pack, withdrew my pill canister, popped two OxyContin, and washed them down with Jack and Coke. "Just a second," I said to my Native American emissaries, all smartly attired and wearing their hair in ponytails, the men as well as the woman, and lit up a menthol cigarette. My pleasure receptors open as baseball mitts, I said, "Okay. I'm ready to be officially told I've won."

"I wish we could, but look," the woman said and with a varnished nail directed my attention to a third wheel that hadn't stopped on canned beans, as I'd assumed, but on campfire logs. "This machine's experiencing a malfunction." Her finger hovered above the payoff chart, there in plain view on the face of the slot machine. "This machine's maximum payoff is two thousand five hundred dollars. There's positively no way for it to pay out more than that without a machine malfunction, and if you'd read the House rules, accessible by punching the House rules key," which, of course, she did, "you'd know the House cannot be held legally responsible for winnings resulting from machine malfunctions of any kind."

"You're telling me I've won a measly two and a half grand?"

"I'm telling you the House cannot be held liable for winnings resulting from machine malfunctions."

"Which means?"

"All the House can do is reimburse you the amount of your bet."

"Five nickels?"

She nodded. "That's wholly righteous," I said.

As the crowd fell away as if from a plague victim, the photographer stepped between my fiancée and me and stationed an accordion-sized camera before the slot machine. He peered into his viewfinder and a white flash went off above my head. When my eyes readjusted to the lighting, the pretty thing to whom I'd pledged my love was gone, mardis gras beads, t-shirt, radioactive sludge and all.

"For your troubles," the female casino manager said, placing a coupon on my lap, "we'll treat you to a dinner-for-two at the casino steakhouse. Does that sound like something you might enjoy?"

"It's better than nothing," I admitted.

I was disappointed, sure, but knew better than to make a mountain out of a molehill. Over the slot machine the pair of male casino managers fit a yellow canvas bag with laces like a straightjacket. On the bag was stenciled "OUT OF ORDER," and as they tightened and knotted cords at the bottom and across the middle, I found myself wishing it were me they had identified and isolated, me they had contained.

At six, I parked beside the curb in front of my daughter's house. In a rust orange sweatshirt and Broncos ball cap, Mike sat on the frame rail of his Peterbilt, the outer tires of which rested on the grass on either side of the driveway. I called to him, "Howdy, Mike," and popped the trunk of my Lincoln. "Mind lending me a hand with the luggage?"

In the mid-90's he'd been signed by Detroit and traded to Denver, where he protected Elway for exactly seven downs before blowing an Achilles', effectively ending his NFL career. On the street I set nine grocery bags of baby clothes Annabel had left when she'd taken the girls to Colorado. As I unloaded a valise, two-suiter, and overnight kit, Mike remained planted above his truck's leaf springs, idly slapping a monkey wrench into his palm. "How thoughtless of me," I said. "You're a father now. Congratulations." With the same winning smile I'd shown presidents when they came to Nevada to see for themselves what species of man they'd employed at the Test Site, I made a bee-line for my son-in-law. "You and Cecily have waited a long time for this. You deserve nothing but joy."

Neither Cecily nor Kate had proven particularly fertile. Both had been diagnosed with hormonal imbalances their doctors had treated with regimens of estrogen, progesterone, and prolactin, but only Cecily had conceived. I'd felt for them, I had. Like their father, both were genetically predisposed to depression, and in an America forever broadcasting to the world its capacity to destroy the world thousands of times over, children gave one hope that the human race's finest attributes would prevail in the end. Without children, we as a nation had nothing to protect, and without a child of one's own, it was easy to believe we as a nation had nothing to lose.

"You carrying any of that radioactive shit on you, Gordon?" Mike asked when I came to a stop before him on the driveway. "Because if you are, I'm going to have to ask you, as nicely as I know how, to cart your skinny ass straight back to Vegas."

I wagged my head, no.

"I don't have a counter, so you're going to have to empty your pockets for me."

"Has J.R.'s ghost taken residence inside your head?" I asked.

"I'm not letting you inside the house until I'm sure you're clean. Simple as that."

"I'm clean," I said, at the same time wishing I weren't, wishing I'd retained the sludge I'd given to the girl who'd vanished from the casino before telling me her name.

Like the sun itself, the subterranean nuclear explosions to which I'd devoted my working life had bolstered my immune system and strengthened my resistance to illnesses. And in the gamma rays still emitted by the souvenirs I'd taken home from the more than 700 tests I'd overseen, they continued to in ever shortening half-lives. Each pit we'd planted had been connected by five, ten, twenty miles of fiber optic cable to mobile units manned by physicists from the nation's top labs, and to me even the nuts and bolts and sections of married wire that had lain just outside the melting range were talismans. Without a remnant from a blast, I felt nervous and vulnerable and no longer as impervious to pressures.

Still Mike was entitled to his opinions, upsetting to me as they were. So I emptied my pockets of change, lighter, wallet, cigarettes, flask, and the coupon from the casino for a steak dinner-for-two and laid everything out on the driveway for Mike to inspect. "Let's see what's in the fanny pack, Gordon," he said from his throne of reinforced steel.

"I'll tell you what's in the fanny pack," I said. "Pills."

"Take 'em out," he replied, so I laid out the vials of OxyContin, Percocet, Vicodin, Valium, Xanax, Demerol, Tylenol 3, and Ambien. Mike set the monkey wrench on his rig's fifth wheel and knelt on the concrete. He picked up each vial and examined the label, his pupils wide as camera shutters. "Sweet Jesus, Gordon," he said when he'd set down my sleep medication, "with all this garbage in your system, it's a wonder you can drive, gamble, or talk on the telephone. It's a wonder you can function at all."

"I have a strong constitution, unlike a certain overeducated prick who recently passed on." I grinned and coughed.

Mike sighed. "You can trash talk J.R. all you like in front of me. Lord knows, I didn't hold him in the highest esteem either. But I'd watch your mouth around Cecily."

"Cecily and I are of like minds about her stepfather."

In spite of the distance separating us, my daughters and I had remained close. Kate conducted research on rocket engines at Boeing and Cecily did clerical work for Sandia. Together they were the second generation of Langleys to earn a living within the country's industrial-military complex, and I was proud of them.

"Be that as it may," Mike said, "Annabel's still in deep grief over J.R., and she only left this morning."

"Annabel was here this morning?" I said.

"Uh-huh. She was here for ten days helping Cecily look after the baby, but I think it was Cecily who had the tougher job looking after her."

"So Annabel was here this morning," I said.

"Pick your pills up off the driveway, and I'll help you with your bags."

With little of the fanfare I'd come to expect from my youngest daughter, Cecily hugged me briskly in the kitchen, then kissed me brusquely on the cheek. Late February, spring was taking its sweet time getting to Albuquerque, and the aromas from the oven put me in mind of families and how grateful I felt to be basking in the warmth of one. Most nights I microwaved a frozen dinner or ate at one of the casinos, and here Cecily had gone to the trouble of preparing a supper of roast chicken, mashed potatoes, biscuits, and gravy. I unscrewed the stopper of my flask and took a nip.

"Now stay put a second, would you, darling? Let me get a look at you." I leaned back against a countertop speckled with radish filings and celery leaves as Cecily smiled coquettishly. "That's my girl," I said, but before the words were out her smile was gone, a radioisotope that had already changed into something else in the time taken to identify it.

"You drink too much, Dad," she said and returned to paring a cucumber over the sink. Though I loved my daughters equally, Cecily was the beauty of the family, with pale white skin and dark brown hair that curled at her shoulders.

"I drink just enough to balance the pills," I replied.

"You take too many pills, too."

"I'm an old man," I said. "The pills help me regulate my environment."

Mike came into the kitchen carrying three bags of baby clothes. "Riddle me this, honey? What do your old man and Rush Limbaugh have in common?"

"I can't believe you spoke of me and him in the same breath," I said. "I can't stand that blatherskite."

"Give up?" Mike said as he dropped three bags of baby clothes on top of the six I'd brought in. "OxyContin."

I unzipped my fanny pack, located my Tylenol 3,

and popped two. "Both of you know the kind of work I did. But do either of you have any idea, any idea at all, of the mental toll testing weapons meant to annihilate hundreds of thousands of people in a matter of seconds takes on the human psyche? Do you? In my lifetime I participated in over seven hundred such tests. And I would do it again, happily and with honor. But it takes its toll, is all I'm saying."

They'd heard it before, but I didn't care. Cecily turned to me with a vegetable peeler in her hand, her creased brow an etched pagoda. "OxyContin is an opioid, Dad."

"Opioids work for me," I replied, "especially in combination with other opioids."

"Opioids are for patients on their deathbeds."

"Maybe I'm on my mine and I don't even know it." I smiled, which made Cecily frown. "Seriously, darling, if you'd seen our subsidence craters, which you haven't because they're off-limits to the public, maybe you'd have an inkling of the enormous destructive capability basically uneducated, God-fearing men like me handled on a bi- and tri-weekly basis."

Mike snorted. "That why you brought all that radioactive shit home with you, Gordon? That why you contaminated an environment you shared with your wife and children? You wanted to spread the suffering around, didn't you? So you wouldn't be the only one with altered DNA, the only one with permanently mutated genes. You wanted to leave your mark on history, didn't you, Gordon?"

Cecily shot her husband a furious glance. "My father didn't know any better. The government gave the men hardhats and sunglasses to wear. That's the message men like my father received."

"And most of us threw our hardhats and sunglasses away," I said, "because the explosions were underground, in case you hadn't heard, and we were protected by hundreds, if not thousands, of feet of solid bedrock. The minute levels of radiation that seeped up through the desert floor weren't dangerous. Few of us even came down with colds. Some tests required a week of eighteen-hour days, which we clocked without suffering the slightest fatigue."

I had no intention of adding to Mike and Cecily's duress. Crescent moons of phantasmagorical purple and brown lay recumbent beneath their eyes. I felt for them, I did. They'd recently brought bawling human life into the world. But this wasn't an argument I expected to have with them. At wedding receptions —I'd attended one for Cecily and two for Kate, whose first marriage ended in divorce— J.R. was the one I quarreled with, his liberalism and belief in social change easily as idiotic as the conservative war-mongering heard 24-7 up and down the AM dial. Now that J.R. was dead, it seemed as if he'd divided, and I wondered if he'd multiplied and the next time I visited Kate and her homosexual second husband Donny, they'd be his ghostly ventriloquist's dummies, too. I thought of the $1,597,244.10 I hadn't won and how different things might've been if only my lovely young fiancée were running interference for me.

"Indeed, thanks to the radiation I received back

then and the ever-diminishing doses I receive at home, I can mix diazepam, hydrocodone, acetaminophen, codeine, anti-insomnia drugs, anti-anxiety drugs, amphetamines, and other analgesics with alcohol and tobacco without experiencing adverse side effects of any kind. So don't talk to me about the dangers of something not even our nation's top physicists and pharmacists fully understand . . ."

I would've gone on an even more impassioned rant if Mike hadn't slumped to the kitchen floor and begun to weep, all three hundred fifty plus pounds of him shuddering in an orange and blue heap beside the butcher block. Cecily fell to her knees before him and massaged his lineman's neck and shoulders. Peering up at me with plaintive eyes, she said, "Our baby has eleven fingers."

Mike heaved even harder. I saw then what this was all about, the driveway search, the chilly reception. They wanted to pin my grandchild's defect, if 'defect' an eleventh finger could even be called, on me. I unzipped my fanny pack, found my Valium, opened the vial, and handed two 2-milligram pills to Cecily. "Give him these," I said and went to the sink to fill a glass with water.

"We don't drink the tap water," she said, "because it contains traces of mercury."

"A little mercury never hurt anyone," I said, but handed her a glass of filtered water poured from a Brita pitcher as Mike regarded the pair of pills in his palm, each imprinted with a heart, as if they were tealeaves. "Take them." I said. "They're your friends."

"I know what they are," Mike said, wiping tears from his whiskered cheeks. "But what I'd like is Percocet."

"Are you sure?" I said, wary of the fluctuations in mood I experienced whenever I was on them. But Mike nodded, so I took back the pills I'd given him and found the ones he preferred. Before I put the Valium away, I offered them to Cecily, figuring she too could use a lift.

"Thanks, but I'm breastfeeding," she said.

"The Valium will be out of your system entirely by this time tomorrow," I said.

"And Mike Junior will have nursed six times by then," she replied.

"Surely you have infant formula."

"Who's going to feed him infant formula at ten p.m.? At two a.m.? At six a.m.? At noon? You?" she said. "Because if I take two Valium, I guarantee you I won't be conscious before this time tomorrow."

"I'll do it," I said.

"You'll stay up all night?"

"And all day tomorrow, too, if need be."

"Don't you need your rest?" she asked.

"When I need my rest, I take sleep medication." A mischievous smile crossed my daughter's lips. "Take them," I said, holding the pills out to her.

"I can't believe I'm accepting prescription drugs from my own father. It would kill Mom."

"It wouldn't kill your mother if she and I were still together, if she hadn't fallen under the sway of that granola-eating, slogan-spouting peacenik, that healthier-than-thou, sand-worshipping, vegetable-loving hypocrite with the bald head, ponytail, bolo tie, hemp slippers, and twin banana yellow Hummers with vanity plates reading 'Thing 1' and 'Thing 2.'"

"Dad," Cecily said, "J.R.'s dead. You don't have to hate him anymore."

I didn't fault Annabel for leaving me, I faulted her for marrying a man whose idea of a romantic night out was protesting nuclear proliferation in a snowstorm and who would've dismantled the nation's entire arsenal given half a chance, blissfully unaware that every livelihood, even his own, was dependent upon a flourishing weapons program. Indeed, I could not have faulted her more were he, instead, of the camp that maintained we needed to blow every country hostile to American interests to kingdom come. Having the biggest, longest nuclear arms meant never having to use them. What punk picked a fight with Jack Dempsey? Joe Louis? Mohammed Ali? That, in a nutshell, was my politics. Beyond that, I believed in love, specifically the human being's inalienable right to give and receive it freely.

But Cecily was correct. My nemesis for over three decades was dead, and Annabel, whom I would've taken back in a second even after all the years apart, was still grieving her loss of him as much as I was my loss of her.

"You ready to meet your grandson?" Cecily asked, and in the warmth emanating from her eyes I saw the Valium exercising its tranquilizing influence.

I thought of the steak dinner-for-two to which I'd treat myself on my way home. "I might live forever, but

I doubt it."

Cecily sighed. "You'll probably outlive us all." As she rose from the kitchen floor, she kissed Mike on the button of his ball cap. "Get up, you big lovable oaf." A mammoth hand closed around her slender wrist—between the second and third knuckle of each finger a skull and crossbones had been tattooed—and she lugged him onto knees the size of small duffle bags. From there Mike raised himself from the linoleum one leg at a time like a weightlifter under a bowing yoke of iron. Once on his feet, he engulfed her in an embrace, and Cecily was a child again, on a Halloween long ago, in a grizzly bear costume that needed zipping up in the back.

A human lean-to, they led me to a master bedroom that smelled of milk, and in a crib canopied with dangling stegosaurs, tyrannosaurs, and triceratops Mike Jr. lay bundled in blankets. "Oh my," I said and gathered my grandson in my arms. To me he seemed the most perfect of creatures, his lids leaf-shaped and so translucent I thought I could see his pupils studying me through the networks of delicate blue veins. I pulled back his swaddling and his arms sprang up as if in surprise, though he remained sleeping. On his right hand were a thumb and five fingers, digits five and six veering out from a shared midcarpal joint like identical necks of a newborn two-headed snake.

"Who knows?" I said. "With his extra finger, maybe he'll be the first to perform Rachmaninoff's 'Second Piano Concerto' the way it was meant to be performed."

"Unh-unh," Mike said. "The little fella's getting a

Stratocaster the day he turns five. I've already exposed him to Jimi, Jimmy, and Frank."

"Who?"

"Hendrix, Page, and Zappa."

Cecily was peeking at her baby over my shoulder, humming "You Are My Sunshine." "The obstetrician asked us whether we wanted the extra finger removed. We told her no."

"Of course you did, sweetheart," I said. "You don't know why he's been given it. Nobody does."

"We almost told her yes."

Soon she and Mike were in the guestroom setting up a bassinet, giggling, neither long for this world.

I understood. Every couple prayed that their baby would be born perfect. But what did 'perfect' mean? If I'd learned anything from my thirty years at the Test Site, it was that we as a race were forever adapting to changes we had wrought upon the earth. Who was to say we weren't entering an age in which eleven fingers was the norm? As I held my first and no doubt only grandchild in my arms, I imagined human beings in the not-so-distant future playing musical instruments that looked nothing like the musical instruments of to-day, with hundreds of keys and thousands of strings and perhaps more than one mouthpiece.

To this day a curious red wildflower springs up on the Test Site after a rain, and it has no name.

81

Connected

Fifteen minutes before sunset a catamaran deposited wedding guests onto sand the white of fine china. Gary remained on the sailboat beside Mel whose gray-black locks hung loose in the tropical humidity. Seven months pregnant, she leaned into him, smelling of the avocado shampoo with which the maid service stocked their bathroom every morning, and something else, citrus-y, lulling. Gary wondered if she'd purchased perfume from the hotel's gift shop that afternoon while he'd zipped around in a borrowed speedboat with Maurice and Maurice's six groomsmen. Elaine's fiancé liked to brag that in his twenties he had apprenticed under the best chefs on Saint Thomas and that in getting married on a secluded beach of Saint John he was realizing a lifelong dream. For days he'd wanted to show his Chicago buddies, and anyone else who would come along, a sunken sport-fishing launch only the locals knew about. It would take two hours, he kept telling people, to get to where a crow's nest stuck up out of the sea like "a lifeguard's chair," and Gary had been on the verge of bowing out when his sister phoned his hotel room to tell him how much it would hurt Maurice, and her, if he did.

"I know you're thinking about not going," Elaine said. "I *know* you. That's why I'm calling."

"I drank too much *Brugal Anejo* at the rehearsal dinner," he told her. "Mel's in the bathroom throwing up. And you want me to go with your fiancé on a boat trip?"

"Uh-huh," she said.

Though he could barely read, Maurice claimed he had never been lost, that taken anywhere in the world he could find his way home without benefit of a map, compass, or money. He was an explorer, an adventurer, a citizen of the world, as comfortable, according to Elaine, taking a friend's Formula One on a trial run as he was talking to diplomats, or men playing chess in the park, on their own turf and in their own language, which he acquired at a conversational level after no more than a half hour's exposure.

"It's astonishing," she had testified to Gary during a break from the Modern Language Association's annual conference, having witnessed with her own eyes and ears Maurice, born and raised in Jefferson Park twenty minutes from O'Hare, carrying on with Cretan farmers at the ruined palace of Cnossus about Marxist politics, with champagne-producers in Epernay about Chirac's foreign and domestic policies, with Alexandrians honeymooning at the pyramids about Israel's occupation of the West Bank.

"Maurice believes in a universal language. According to him, the less one knows about any single tongue the more open one is to speech in all its varieties. I've never seen anything like it, Gair. His mind's a steel trap. Everything he hears stays there. It doesn't matter what language it's spoken in. It's as if he's able to extrapolate all the rules of any language's grammar from a few snippets of overheard speech."

Gary and she had taken a cab to a French seafood restaurant in Georgetown. They were sitting in a booth by a window that looked onto Wisconsin Avenue. "And he's illiterate?"

"He reads 'Doonsbury' at breakfast. It takes him between five and ten minutes, but he reads the entire strip. Then he asks me to quiz him on it."

Gary laughed. They were English professors, he at the University of Minnesota, she at De Paul, with a devilishly witty mother who'd instilled a love of tropes in them each before she'd died. As Elaine told him about her plans for a January wedding, a little over a year away, the corners of her mouth turned up, forming adorable quotation marks on her cheeks. He hadn't seen her this animated since before their mother's funeral. She and Maurice had returned from a five-day "reconnaissance mission" to Saint Thomas, and the sun and humidity had imbued her skin with a lush radiance. With her wheat-colored hair knotted loosely à la concierge and crystal earrings refracting glare from the street, she looked the part of an academician and didn't, and he could see why the courses she taught on Restoration Comedy were popular with the rugby team. In a restaurant overrun by pedants, she was easily the most captivating creature there, and as their waiter removed their salad plates Gary ordered another bottle of Sancerre. Neither were delivering papers, their search committees had finished interviewing post-docs, and their departments would cover their bouillabaisse and profiteroles.

"So is Dad paying for the wedding?" he asked.

"Twenty grand was all he could afford, but Maurice told him no."

"You're flying seventy people to the Virgin Islands and putting them up at the Hyatt for five nights, Bing."

"Maurice's uncle is paying for everything."

"Maurice's uncle?"

"Julio. I haven't met him. But I know what you're thinking."

"Is he—?"

"No." Elaine was adamant. "And now I want you to promise me something."

"What?"

"That from this moment on you'll keep such thoughts to yourself. Maurice is sensitive about his heritage. When I asked him the same question you just asked me, he looked so wounded I thought he was going to cry."

"What's his uncle's line? Import-export?"

Elaine frowned. "I have no idea. Maurice doesn't either. All I know is that I've never been happier in my life."

Gary could see that what she said was true and at thirty-seven she wasn't getting any younger.

"Do you promise?" she said.

"I do."

Maurice cut the engine and tied the speedboat to the tower of the sunken launch. The site was breathtaking, the stuff of travel agency brochures. Under a fiberglass canopy ciliated with antennae and speckled with gull droppings a fish-fighting chair, its cushions eroded away, was stationed three feet above their very own jade expanse of Caribbean Sea. The balance of the sunken vessel lay on the edge of a coral reef that Maurice encouraged the others to explore with snorkels and masks as he knelt on the deck and fiddled with the pressure gauge of an oxygen tank. Having logged over eight hundred diving hours Maurice wasn't about to miss this opportunity.

Gary studied a nautical map laminated onto a tabletop in the cockpit, identified what he thought were Virgin Gorda, Tortola, Anegada, hazy green landmasses that floated in the distance. Never would he come here again. About how many places could one say that? His forty-second birthday fell within a week of Mel's due date. Soon his life would change for the better. In the last five years she and he had fought more, if "fighting" it could be called. Usually without any precipitating event he could identify she would withdraw from him, and for two weeks to a month they would occupy the same living space, the entire third floor of a red brick three-story apartment building across the street from Loring Park in Minneapolis, but effectually lead separate lives, she leaving for work (and her morning workout at the gym) at 6 a.m., he lingering about the condo resuming articles where he'd left off on them the day before and grading essays until early afternoon when he taught "British Romantic Poetry: Blake to Shelley." Then, just as suddenly, she would approach him trembling—recently it had happened on a Saturday afternoon when he was making Malt-O-Meal for himself, another time when the Vikings were losing a Monday night game to the Packers on TV—and burst into tears, claiming everything that bound them (an apartment building upon which they paid equal shares of the mortgage, and so many furnishings, from furniture to appliances and consoles to books, CDs, and art, the very thought of dividing it up took her breath away) was false. They'd lost what love they'd had, sacrificed it on the pyre of human comforts, torched it in the process of eliminating danger from their lives. Each had provided the stability the other needed to excel professionally, but once she'd made partner at her architectural firm and he awarded tenure, it was as if they'd forgotten they'd put a baby in the bath.

Now they were having a real one, a girl if the ultrasounds were trustworthy, and Gary felt as if they'd been given a second chance. With emails from babycenter.com updating them weekly on the development of the fetus, Lamaze classes, and a library of books on pregnancy, childbirth, infant care, and childrearing, they were no longer at a loss for things to talk about. If most of their single friends had distanced themselves as if from an enormous conversation processor that pureed the brains of all who entered it, their married friends, even the childless ones, had rallied behind them, a few even foregoing wine at dinner parties and all eager to share with them what they had learned by becoming parents themselves or anxious to hear what might, God willing, await them too.

When all but one of Maurice's groomsmen had flipped backward from the gunwales into the sea, Maurice produced a mask and snorkel from his duffle bag and handed them to Gary. "This is much better equipment than what I gave those bozos." He thumbed over his shoulder at five fluorescent orange rings bobbing like detritus around what looked, Gary had to admit, much like a lifeguard's chair. "And here, my man, is a pair of most excellent flippers. They might be a little big on you, bro, but give 'em a try. My guess is, three kicks and you'll be outside the galley staring into the eyes of the giant man-eating octopus that makes it her home."

"There's a giant man-eating octopus down there?" asked Stephano whose wife, Cindy, was pregnant, too, and even bigger than Mel.

"Dude," Maurice exclaimed. "Many an unlucky diver has discovered firsthand the tremendous strength of her tentacles. But I made my peace with her long ago and she bestowed upon me all the diving gear left behind after she'd sucked the last remnants of human flesh from it."

Maurice winked at Gary and smiled broadly, goofily. "You can tell Stephano anything and he'll believe it. Three years ago he came to Chicago from Bolzano, at the base of the Italian Alps, where he spent his winters skiing and his summers yodeling. Now he owns a popular nightclub in Cicero. Five nights a week he books hip-hop artists, jazz musicians, rock-a-billy groups, you name it. But sophistication for Stephano is just a guise. Beneath his Gucci sunglasses and Joseph Abboud beachwear is a simple peasant."

If Gary was a head taller than Stephano, Maurice

was a head taller than Gary, and the effect of Maurice grabbing Stephano's face in his hands and planting kisses on either cheek was similar, Gary thought, to a giraffe nibbling leaves from the ground. When he was through Maurice turned to Gary. "If Stephano asks to use the flippers, mask, and snorkel I've given you as a gift for being a most excellent brother-in-law-to-be, you mustn't let him, Gair."

Maurice heaved the oxygen tank onto his back, then fastened black rubber straps over his shoulders and across his chest and waist. "Stephano can't swim. Of course he wants people to *think* he can, which is why he spends all day wading in the shallow end of the hotel pool."

"Not true," Stephano exclaimed. "I spend all day wading because I want to *learn* to swim." Stephano smiled weakly. "But Maurice is right about one thing. If I ask to use your flippers, mask, and snorkel, you mustn't let me, Gair, for my lungs will fill with water and I will swiftly drown." Maurice and Stephano laughed and kissed. Then Maurice sat down on a gunwale, affixed his diving mask to his face, and slipped into the sea.

"You should join him," Stephano said, squatting before an ice chest filled with Perrier and beer. From a corner of the chest he withdrew a bottle of the unbelievably smooth Dominican rum Gary had sampled more than once the night before. Stephano dropped an ice cube into a plastic tumbler, poured two fingers of the caramel liquid over it, and held it before him like a divining crystal.

"If I were you, Gair, I would snorkel with the others. At our home in Chicago Cindy and I have installed a ninety-gallon aquatic environment which, I am happy to say, is home to many varieties of anthia, butterfly-fish, triggerfish, dragonets, surgeonfish, lionfish, goby, and wrasse, in addition to many varieties of coral, star-fish, and other invertebrates. And I must say that after suffering yet another tension-filled evening at the club, nothing brings me peace like the perfect quiet to be found only at the bottom of the sea, which I have tried to replicate in the twenty-second floor apartment Cindy and I share. But unfortunately Cindy does not share my amoré for tropical fish. Indeed she loathes them. And so it is a great injustice and gross irony that I, Stephano, lover of the redlip blenny, Atlantic blue tang, spiny puffer, spotted goatfish, blacktail dascyllus, flamefish, and highhat, must remain above sea level while those with a more Cindy-like regard for crea-tures of the deep may journey below to gawk at what to them must seem like nothing more than freakish aberrations of nature."

Against his better judgment, Gary poured himself some rum. His sister believed Maurice, his business associates, friends, and relatives 100% legitimate. Mel, whose grandparents had emigrated from Sicily to New York in the Twenties, was equally certain they were not. "You and Elaine need to pull your heads out of your asses," she'd said after meeting Maurice once at a dinner he'd thrown for them at his restaurant in North Park. They'd flown to Chicago in late September to cel-ebrate the baby and wedding, and no sooner had they seated themselves than Maurice produced a grilled rack-of-lamb for them each and garlic mashed potatoes served family style. Though Mel wasn't drinking, he produced a bottle of 1987 Brunello di Montalcino from his cellar and, afterward, brought out cappuccinos and zabaglione semifreddo. "You and your sister may be experts at discerning subtleties in texts, but when it comes to seeing what's right in front of your faces, I swear you're each missing a gene."

She might have indicted their father too, a New Critic who'd studied under Cleanth Brooks at Vanderbilt in the Fifties before assuming a teaching post at the University of Michigan in 1963. Gary wasn't disagreeing with her. He was simply keeping the promise he'd made to Elaine in D.C. Who was he to say Maurice and his groomsmen *weren't* connected? None was over thirty-five, none had gone to college, all knew one another from bussing and waiting tables at restaurants namedropped like prestigious alma maters; now all owned restaurants, with the exception of Stephano, who owned a nightclub.

"You must be very excited about the baby," Gary said, not the strongest swimmer either, nor of the opinion that one needed to *see* natural wonders to visualize them and pleased Stephano and he had, beyond a shared taste for rum, imminent fatherhood in common.

"Oh yes," Stephano exclaimed. "I almost cannot bear to talk about it I am so excited. Can you imagine me, Stephano, a father? I almost . . . how do you say? I almost cannot wrap my brain around it. There, I said it."

"I know," said Gary. "Me neither."

"And yet," said Stephano, "it is very scary, is it not? Soon we two men, we two overgrown *boys*, shall have delicate babies in our care. We who do not even know how to properly care for ourselves will be entrusted with the lives of infants. *Human* infants. It is very lucky for us, lucky for the entire human race, that women are so much smarter than us."

He gestured off the side of the speedboat at the other groomsmen's bobbing, spurting snorkels.

"Have they not seen *Jaws One, Two, Three*, and *Jaws: The Revenge*? What would they do in the event of a shark attack? What would *we* do? I have no navigational ability. I cannot operate a speedboat. My life would be entirely in your hands, Gair, and you do not strike me as a Roy Scheider."

Gary had to laugh. "And yet," Stephano continued, "if only I knew how to swim I would be out there, too, manly flipping my flippers, blowing water through my blow-hole, putting my life, my wife and as-yet-unborn son's well-being in harm's way and for what? I ask you."

Some lines of Keats, from *Endymion*, "Book I," returned to him:

> There blossom'd suddenly a magic bed
> Of sacred ditamy, and poppies red . . .

—and at first Gary could not say why. *Endymion* wasn't his favorite of Keats' book-length poems, not by a long shot, and in survey courses he treated it as a footnote to the more complicated and, to most critics' minds, richer *Hyperion*, excerpts of which he taught as preludes to "The Eve of St. Agnes," "Ode on a Grecian Urn," "Ode to a Nightingale," "La Belle Dame Sans Merci," and "Lamia," which, to his mind, were the five best poems Keats committed to paper and among the best poems in the English language. Then he remembered, at Princeton, in graduate school, during his oral exams, a member of his Committee on Studies had asked him what "ditamy" was. "A flower," he replied and the professor asked, "What type?" Gary supplied the proper name, *dittany*, for the poeticized one, which displeased the professor who afterward explained that the *Rutaceae* known as fraxinella was, in fact, what Keats had had in mind, a flower that in hot weather emitted a flammable vapor and in classical mythology was reputed to expel arrows from the body. "If Endymion," the professor argued, "has been punctured by Cupid's arrow and fallen in love with the Goddess of the Moon, it's fraxinella the poor chap needs, not dittany, for Christ's sake."

Dittany? Fraxinella? What difference did it make? Later celebrating at the bar, Gary narrated the incident to classmates, recasting the professor's mellifluous British accent as a guttural German one and portraying him as a Gestapo interrogator. Pedantry was so easy to skewer back then, yet somehow against his will, having again and again renewed his vows to eschew the obsession with minutia that crippled the study of literature and sentenced its relevancy to death, he'd become its high priest. In twenty years he might well find himself

93

questioning some poor graduate student's knowledge of botany and not with a German or even British accent, but in his own boring Midwestern one.

"Know what?" he said. "I'm going in."

"I envy you," said Stephano.

"And I you," Gary replied.

"We should join the wedding party," Gary said and Melissa sighed. Practically from the moment of their baby's conception she'd been sick. "I'll be with you every step of the way, honey."

A narrow stairwell led from the catamaran's main deck to its portside pontoon, lodged in submerged sand twenty feet from where a feathery line of froth lapped the beach. The guests were barefoot, the men in slacks soaked to their upper calves in spite of having rolled their pant legs to their knees. Soaked to the knees were the khakis of his father, the literary critic whose name he shared and who at seventy-eight was no longer the robust renegade Gary remembered but who was nonetheless waving at them as frantically as he might've were they disembarking from the Queen Elizabeth's maiden voyage. The chaplain, who'd driven his car onto the ferry at Red Hook and stood in dry vestments against a backdrop of palm trees, was calling for witnesses to gather in a semicircle around the bride and groom, upon whose shoulders he'd stationed his hands as if to keep the couple from wandering off. Gary lowered himself from the pontoon into the water, felt sand and seashell shards scrambling under his soles like hermit crabs. Perhaps they were hermit crabs, a whole colony.

He held Mel's hand as she sat down on the float in a Dresden blue blouse and miniskirt he'd helped her pick out at an upscale maternity shop in Edina. As he slid his arms under her thighs and around her waist, she wrapped her arms around his neck, and again he detected the fragrance—lemony, exotic—he'd smelled when the sailboat had first left port and she'd returned from the head having puked for the eighth time that day. As terrible as she felt, she was making an effort, and he prayed that with all the weight she'd put on he wouldn't stumble.

"Upsy daisy, Mel."

"Just remember, Gary," she said, "all this beauty, all this romance—it's paid for in blood."

"We don't know that," he replied.

"Maybe you don't."

"Look," he said as he set her feet first on the sand, "it's as if I carried you across the threshold."

"It doesn't mean we're married," she said.

"Where's the harm in pretending, sweetheart," he replied. "We've lived together ten years. We're having a baby."

That quickly his father was upon them wiping tears from his eyes with a black handkerchief. "I wish Martha were alive. She would love this. Look at Elaine. Isn't she lovely?"

Elaine *was* lovely in their mother's ankle-length brocaded wedding gown, replete with Gainsborough hat, veil, point d'appliqué, and jabot, and Gary couldn't help thinking that if their mother had lived to see this she would've loved the intrigue without disparaging the entire ceremony. Over the shoulders of two attractive, olive-skinned women in their twenties, one wearing her hair in a chignon with blond streaks, the other in corkscrews the blue of carnival glass, Gary caught his sister's eye and thought she smiled at him. In two years she and Maurice had traveled twice to Europe, once to the Middle East, and twice to the Virgin Islands, and hadn't paid for their globetrotting on her Associate Professor's salary, that was for sure. But while it had never occurred to him, or Mel, or probably Elaine either, that success might lie at the end of any other path than one that led through a succession of ivory towers, a wall of framed diplomas wasn't everyone's press pass. A G.E.D., if that's what Maurice held, wasn't slowing him down. In addition to owning Spoleto, he operated a catering company, Aperitivo, which specialized in canapés. No doubt Maurice worked very hard. And yet—it was as if Mel were arguing with him inside his head—so did lots of people who couldn't afford Porsches or Harleys, and Maurice had one of each. How many busboys, he could almost hear her asking him, grew up to be five-star restaurateurs?

"Doesn't all this make you two want to tie the knot?" his father asked. "All this beauty? All this romance?"

Melissa coughed. "If Mel and I tie the knot," Gary answered, "it won't be on Saint Thomas *or* Saint John."

"No, of course not," his father replied. "Your mother and I were married in a red brick church in Jackson, Tennessee, though we were both atheists."

"I know," Gary said. "You did it to appease her Episcopalian parents."

"And my Methodist ones. If you think either one of us wanted to go through life having defied our mothers and fathers you're sadly mistaken."

Gary laughed. While his mother lived his father had remained mute on the subject of their children's marital status, but when she died she handed him the baton. "Is that what Mel and I are doing? Defying you?"

"Your mother wanted you to get married," his father said. "You know that."

"Mom's dead," Gary replied. "Her wishes can hardly be said to matter, can they?"

"Your mother's here," his father said. "She's by my side."

"What happened to your cherished nihilism, Pops? Your beloved absurdist philosophy?"

"Nihilism, absurdist philosophy, these are young men's follies. For an old man to cling to them is just pig-headed. Your mother's here, Gary."

"But your life's work? Does this mean you based all of it on a false premise?"

"In academia everyone's work is based on a false premise."

"Here, here," Mel said and his father cackled.

"You just don't know it," his father added, "until you're finished."

Gary wasn't so sure. For years he'd doubted the "truth" of what he was doing. The articles he wrote, no matter how apostate, were read by scholars of British Romanticism and no one else. While he could claim to have turned on at least one undergraduate student

97

per semester for as long as he'd taught at the university, what had he really done for them? Instilled in them a passion for the esoteric? Consigned them to library stacks and, if they went on to study at the graduate level and bore up under pressure as intense as medical school, five figure salaries at best? While he could tell himself he was teaching his students to *read*, to experience a poem by Wordsworth or Coleridge as they might a transformative event in their lives, how many transformative events could one endure without becoming numb? The more deeply one read, which was to say the more fluently one discoursed with the British Romantics on their own terms and in their own language, the more one isolated oneself from contemporaries, spouses, friends, departmental colleagues whose fervor for literature rarely extended beyond their own specialties. Might his father be willing at last to side with Kant and concede that the corporeal world was, as the British Romantics posited, *noumenal*? He wanted to ask, but feared the groan from Mel who in ten years had lost her stomach for the entire Western Canon, from *Beowulf* to Tolstoy, and read, when she read at all, chick lit.

The chaplain announced, "The groom may kiss the bride," and Maurice, grinning, lifted Elaine's veil, and then she was subsumed by the wide back of his tuxedo, pulsating under camera flashes. In the time it had taken them to exchange marriage vows, the sun had set and the trunks of palm trees shimmered pink. When Maurice faced the crowd he and Elaine beamed, their cheeks glistening, and it seemed to Gary as if every couple but Mel and he were locked in an embrace. He took her hand in his, but when he turned to kiss her, it was as if she could tell that the impulse, if "impulse" it could even be called, had been arrived at by deduction. Then he closed his eyes and kissed her anyway.

The next morning Gary breakfasted on coconut pancakes and sausage sweetened with mango at the hotel's beachfront restaurant, a veranda thatched with palm fronds. In the cove the water was choppy, and thirty-seven sailboats—Gary had counted the masts while waiting for the aspirin he'd swallowed with his orange juice to take effect—tugged against their anchor lines. In the *USA Today* slipped under his room door, he scanned the high and low temperatures for major American cities, then read about the arctic cold front stalled over Minneapolis-St. Paul, where the low that night was expected to be 25 below, 60 below with the wind chill. Three years before he had reinsulated all the water pipes of the apartment building, and before leaving for the airport had given the number of the hotel to the tenants on the first and second floors, and still he felt as if he ought to have been at home, even if doing nothing more than putting the finishing touches on the first chapter of a book he had begun about the symbolic use of children in British Romantic Poetry. It was scholarship inspired by a passage from the too often neglected Thomas de Quincey essay, "Literature of Knowledge and Literature of Power"—

"What is the effect . . . upon society, of children?
By the pity, by the tenderness, and by the pecu-

liar modes of admiration, which connect themselves with the helplessness, with the innocence,
and with the simplicity of children, not only are
the primal affections strengthened and continually renewed, but the qualities which are dearest
in the sight of heaven—the frailty, for instance,
which appeals to forbearance, the innocence
which symbolizes the heavenly, and the simplicity which is most alien to the worldly—are kept
up in perpetual remembrance, and their ideals
are continually refreshed."
—and the forthcoming arrival of his daughter.

At a table by himself at a far corner of the veranda sat
Julio, the old man who'd single-handedly made Maurice and Elaine's elaborate wedding possible. Gary had
been introduced to him at the rehearsal dinner and noticed him again at the wedding and later at the reception, held at a Venetian bistro in Charlotte Amalie to
which, upon stepping from the catamaran onto a dock,
all seventy guests had been whisked in open-air bus-
ses. The night was a whirl, fragmented by the nonstop
motion, alcohol consumption, exhaustion, and mer-
riment, but in almost every shard Gary could see the
old man's bald pate and wizened features back lit and
always at some remove, as if he were taking quiet satis-
faction in his creation. For two years Maurice's mother
had been widowed, his father having died of a heart attack in the bathroom shaving within months of taking
out a life insurance policy worth 2.5 million dollars,
and her grief, according to Elaine, had exacerbated her
dementia such that she now required around-the-clock

medical attention. If Julio were, as a point of honor or out of familial obligation, assuming his brother's role, it was funny he had made no toast, nor was he cited in the toasts of any of the others, which had gone on and on with even a distant aunt tinkling her water goblet and sharing stories about Maurice at four, at six, at ten.

As Julio's coffee cup was refilled Gary imagined the waiter putting a revolver to Julio's temple, then laughed at himself for having fallen under Mel's cynical spell. Was it not human nature to suspect the worst of people? Gary returned to his paper, and when he glanced up Maurice stood beside his uncle's table in his orange swimming trunks. At his feet rested his oxygen tanks and duffle bag. When Maurice was finished speaking he turned to leave, then strode across the veranda to Gary.

"I have very sad news, my friend. Stephano is missing. We think he may have drowned last night." Maurice gestured at the cove, at the moored hulls slapping the sea. Though the sky was clear, the wind carried sand across the water and a brown haze hung suspended above the white caps. "Some of us are forming a search party."

"Why would he go swimming," Gary asked, "when he doesn't know how to?"

"He was drunk," Maurice replied, "and his nightclub isn't meeting profit margins. According to Cindy, after his toast that made everyone laugh so hard at the reception, he became morose, and afterward in their hotel room they argued about the baby, making ends meet, his unhappiness at being responsible for a struggling nightclub, everything. That's when he grabbed the snorkeling gear he's been using everyday in the pool, bent over for hours with his mask to the water like some crazy, lovable, full-blown idiot. You've seen him, Gair."

Gary nodded. "You think it was suicide?"

Maurice rubbed his eyes with his fists. "I don't want to speculate. I just want to find him. The groomsmen are meeting on the beach in ten minutes with their fins, masks, and snorkels. We'll form a dragnet. Will you help us?"

"Of course."

Gary signaled for his check, slapped his room number at the bottom of it. Julio was even covering incidentals. Still in her maternity slip from the night before, Mel lay on their bed watching three women in leotards perform an aerobic routine on television. Gary handed her the Styrofoam container he'd brought back for her. In it was the breakfast she'd requested: two poached eggs, English muffin and marmalade, fruit cup, heavy on the red grapes which supposedly contained something that did something for the developing fetus.

"Training by osmosis?" he asked, to which she chose not to respond. "I ran into Maurice. Apparently, Stephano went snorkeling at four this morning and nobody's seen him since."

"Stephano Maurice's groomsman? He doesn't know how to swim. He's the one who stands for hours in the shallow end of the pool."

"He adores tropical fish. He told me all about it yesterday on the speedboat."

"A lot of tropical fish he's going to see at night." Mel popped an ice cube into her mouth from the bowl on her nightstand.

"Feeling any better?"

"A little," she said.

Gary retrieved his swimming trunks from the shower and put them on in the bathroom. He grabbed a towel and the snorkeling gear Maurice had given him as a present.

"I could've told you something like this would happen," Mel said. "Your sister has no idea what she's gotten herself into. No idea. She's a fool. You're *both* fools."

He'd been about to ask her about the scent she'd worn to the wedding, to tell her of the effect it had had on him, when suddenly he knew the scent would never affect him the same way again.

What, he asked himself, would become of their poor daughter?

Maurice was organizing the groomsmen in a line on the sand when Gary arrived. "Let's bow our heads and pray that Stephano is sleeping off his drunk in some drunk girl's hotel room."

"Amen," one of the groomsmen replied.

"The tide's coming in and the water visibility is poor. I want you to keep thirty to fifty feet between you if you can. We'll swim in a serpentine formation. We should be able to cover the cove in three or four sweeps."

The men spanned out along the beach, Gary among them, and advanced in a line into the surf, scanning left to right for a hand, a foot, a clump of hair to stick

103

up out of waves that rose to their knees, their waists. Gary pulled his mask over his eyes, bit down on his snorkel's mouthpiece, and dove into water that seemed colder than it had the day before. What he'd seen beneath the surface had been magical, a sport fishing launch at rest on a coral reef as if placed there by God. As he'd descended through columns of refracted light into the wreck, he'd barely thought about the people who'd been onboard the vessel, about whether they'd lived or died, but now as he peered through his lens into a disturbed concoction of froth and sand, he wondered why he hadn't, why he'd felt as if he were in an enormous aquarium where everything—the pilot-house, the galley, an eight-foot-long yellow-spotted eel, a sea anemone, a clownfish, a school of rust-colored, blue-striped groupers, even, oddly enough, himself—had been planted by design. He'd watched Maurice, a bubbling, comforting, stationary presence, and the groomsmen flitting like diving birds to see what strange prize he'd chipped from the ocean floor with his knife and held in his gloves, and could imagine being watched, perhaps by someone like Stephano in his living room late at night.

As Gary zigzagged out into the cove with the others, he had to glance periodically above the surface to reorient himself. Underwater his visibility extended no more than a dozen feet and he worried he was straying from the formation. Probably they all were, and if Stephano were out there, which he doubted, in their dragnet were plenty of holes through which a body might slip. The farther out he swam the more difficult seeing the bottom became and the more physical exertion it required. For twenty or thirty seconds he would hold his breath and swim to within a yard of the ocean floor, but each time he came up for air large tracts receded into a green blur, and he could only guess where he'd left off when he dove again. Soon he was swimming beneath the sailboats, their anchor lines slanting before him in the filtered light like shafts of bamboo, rudders and keels above him like inverted shark fins. His stomach was cramping. He'd been stupid to enter the water so soon after eating. He clung to gunwales to catch his breath, pulled himself along anchor lines to the ocean floor and back. It was as he was pulling himself up one anchor line that he spotted a human form entangled in another several feet away, a dark mass wafting in the celadon haze like a tattered pirate's flag. He surfaced for air and swam to it. That the body could be Stephano's seemed impossible, and as he examined the flipper and distended ankle about which the tide had somehow cinched the rope, the bloated limbs and torso, the mouthpiece inserted between the bulging lips, the mask magnifying the bulbous eyes and dilated pupils, he thought at first he'd discovered another drowning victim. He rose to the surface and returned to the corpse. This time there was no mistaking the brown and white swimming trunks that Stephano had worn on the speedboat and in the pool. Were he to remove them, the label would show that they were Joseph Abboud, of this he was certain.

An accident? Suicide? Murder? The truth almost didn't matter. Gary heaved himself onboard the sailboat and sat down on the deck. The search party had become so spread out and disorganized he couldn't make out a single snorkel. The wind whipped grit against his skin. His lungs contracted and expanded, his muscles ached, but he felt surprisingly well. He'd forgotten to apply sunscreen, and his shoulders and neck would probably blister on the flight home.

On the strip of beachfront a crowd had assembled. No doubt Cindy stood among the gathered, and when he dragged her husband onto the sand he could expect to be beaten. He could expect to be beaten again when he told Mel that he would leave her, but for now he was a hero.

Pleased to Meet Me

I

In a world forever re-creating itself in the image of it-self seen on screens, the shift from100% cotton jeans to those made of 93% synthetic fiber went undetected by Wurst until he arrived at the second of two murder scenes in which the female victim had been wearing a pair at the time of her death. She and her Pinarello CX Carbon Cyclocross lay mangled across the South Bosque bike trail, the toes of her bike shoes still clipped to the pedals. A single bullet, yet to be discovered by Ballistics, had penetrated her temple a little below her sport helmet, and the force of the blast had twisted her from her bicycle seat. The bike's rear tire was pressed up between her legs, and Wurst noted that while the fabric of her jeans resembled denim, it adhered to her skin like ink.

Beyond the crowd of onlookers rose the city's BioPark and Zoo. Too far away to tell if its eyes were open or closed, a polar bear luxuriated on a prefab ledge, its head resting on crossed forepaws. The shot had been fired by a skilled marksman from somewhere within the stand of cottonwoods and salt cedars that sloped to the river. That or the shooter had been lucky. Blood spatters on the weeds and in the dirt indicated that the victim had been traveling between forty and fifty miles per hour at the moment of impact. Wurst stepped over police tape. To Rochelle of the Tethered

Locks, he said, "Have dinner with me tonight."

"Is that a command or an invitation?" she asked.

"An invitation."

"Then afraid I can't," she said. Wurst stared at the stones, bottle glass, and snakeweed surrounding her sensible, black-laced brogans until he drew a laugh from her. "I really can't, Charlie. My sister's on Fall Break and our mother's planned a big to-do, invited all the aunts, uncles, nieces, nephews, and cousins, and she'd kill me if I missed it."

"Kill you?" he said.

"You know what I mean. Jen's the first de la Madrid to go to college, and it's very important to Mama that all of us be in attendance."

Rochelle smiled in a way that told him that nothing had changed, that as fond as she was of him his marital status—divorced—age—fifty—and seven-year-old daughter were deal-breakers. They'd gone on two dates, the first to the Apothecary, an upscale cocktail lounge in a defunct-psychiatric-hospital-turned-three-star-hotel, the second to a rodeo in Socorro. On the drive back from the rodeo, after an afternoon spent cheering barrel racers and bronco riders and while listening to The Replacements on the CD player, in a spirit of full disclosure he offered the details of his child custody arrangement.

"I get Tara on Tuesdays and Saturdays," he said, "in addition to paying her mother five hundred a month to cover dance lessons, childcare, babysitters, what have you. It isn't ideal, I'll grant you that, but Clair and I have things worked out pretty well. At least neither of us is threatening to take the other to court anytime soon."

Out the driver's side window the Gallinas and Datil mountain ranges could have been ocean liners passing before an erupting volcano. A silver earring in the shape of a hand-grenade caught the blood-orange sunset and reflected it back to him through her hair. To see it down was worth what he'd paid for their admissions, Navajo tacos and beer. A rosary bead necklace disappeared in a slender V beneath her camouflaged tank top and he found himself envious of the crucified Christ at the vertex. Rochelle was twenty-nine, too young for him even by the French calculation, and a homicide detective under his supervision to boot, which added as much to his wooziness as his wonderment.

"What would make the arrangement ideal, Charlie?" she asked.

"Clair dead." It was a joke, but he wasn't a comedian, and wouldn't have attempted anything so deadpan if not for the beer. "What I mean," he said, "is that then I could have Tara seven days a week."

Rochelle sighed. "No need to backpedal," she said, and he conceded to her how painful his divorce had been, how hurt feelings had brought the monsters in both Clair and him to the fore, but how in spite of their mutual disdain they'd protected their daughter from the worst of their conflagration. "Hell," he said, "if Clair were in my place, she'd probably tell you she wished *me* dead."

"Don't worry," Rochelle said. "I'm not judging you."

But when they reached the city she wanted to be taken back to her south valley apartment, and although it was only a little after seven on a Sunday evening, she was out of his Firebird before he could ask to walk her to her door. Three months had passed since then, and although he'd asked her out a dozen times, she'd presented him a dozen excuses—a niece's birthday party, a nephew's confirmation, a ground breaking ceremony for a new condominium complex on an uncle's west side property. The de la Madrid clan was old and ubiquitous, and competing against it was like sparring with an octopus, an obligation she couldn't refuse at the end of every tentacle.

"The pants the victim was wearing," Wurst said then. "Aren't they the same type that other female murder victim was wearing, the one we found in the gym parking lot a few weeks back. They look like jeans but they aren't. They're something else."

"Think you've discovered a link, Detective Wurst?" Rochelle asked.

"I don't know," he replied. "It might be a coincidence."

"They're called 'jeggings,'" she said. "A cross between jeans and leggings."

"Am I the only one who doesn't know this?" Wurst asked.

Rochelle told him to step back from the crowd of spectators. "How many women do you see standing around the crime scene?" she asked.

"You want me to count them?"

She nodded. Wurst counted fifteen, most of them

college students. "Now how many of them are wearing jeans?" she asked.

More than half appeared to be, some in sweaters and fleece vests, others in hoodies and jackets, and the women's outerwear pricked him with the thought of Christmas, the saddest of all holidays, looming before him with its appeals to spend and false promises of mirth, its fatiguing buildup, arrival, and aftermath, the lost receipts that complicated gift returns, the disappointments that lasted until the middle of January. There was a reason so many of the aged passed away on the day or just after. In his case, Clair would take Tara away to Albany, New York, as she did every winter holiday, until after New Year's, and then he and his daughter would celebrate a grim, belated Christmas on a Tuesday night once school was back in session.

"Eight or nine?" he said.

"Wrong," Rochelle replied. "None of them are. See how the pants cling to their rear ends. Even designer jeans don't fit as snugly as that."

"So these are 'in' right now, is what you're saying?" Wurst said.

Rochelle shrugged. "Well, you won't see me in a pair," she said.

II

His daughter was wearing a pair when he picked her up from jazz dance class the following Tuesday. She called them skinny jeans, said all her friends were wearing them, and was surprised he hadn't commented on them before if he didn't like them. In the arrangement they'd worked out with the court, Clair was responsible for clothing, and apparently Tara had been wearing them for months without his even noticing. "Regular jeans are too restrictive, Dad," she said. "I can't dance in them."

"Back in my day, we danced in them just fine," he replied. "Of course, they had to be broken in."

"Not the story about The Replacements playing in your high school gym," she said.

"I thought you liked that story," he said.

"I don't hate it," she said. "It's just that I've heard it a thousand times."

Tara sat in the passenger seat of his unmarked squad car, her iCarly backpack scrunched on the floor between knockoff Uggs that sheathed her calves in faux leather to the knees. Later, when she went missing, he would remember this conversation, how her pants were alerting him to danger. Though true she'd heard some of his story more than once, she hadn't heard it all, and *how many*, he wanted to ask, *could say they'd seen The Replacements for free at a tenth grade sock hop*? The part she hadn't heard, about making out with Loren McGibbon in a storage room on a bed of volleyball nets while Paul, Bob, Tommy, and Chris screamed "Gary's Got a Boner" on the other side of the door, she wouldn't hear from him.

"You know what they look like to me?" he said. "Cartoon jeans. Jeans worn by a cartoon character."

"That's good, right?" she said. "Because cartoons are funny and funny is good." Her flaxen hair surrounded her heart-shaped face like a lion's mane. Since infancy she'd been turning heads, and he didn't imagine it changing when she reached puberty. *Au contraire*, as Rochelle was fond of saying.

"Unh-unh," he said. "Not good. Like Dora the Explorer jeans."

"Dora the Explorer doesn't wear jeans," Tara corrected him. "She wears shorts."

"Then like Bratz jeans," he said. "Like jeans worn by those awful teenaged girls called Bratz."

"Oh yeah," she said with glee. "I see what you're saying. They do, you're right."

"You like wearing jeans that make you look like a cartoon character from the waist down?"

"I wish I could look like a cartoon character from the waist up, too," she replied. "I wish I could *be* a cartoon character."

"Oh yeah?" he said. "Which?"

"Patrick Star," she replied. "On SpongeBob SquarePants."

At home he made spaghetti while Tara sat at the kitchen table studying spelling words. The tests were on Fridays and she scored one hundred percent on them if she practiced during the week, but not if she didn't, which was a point of contention between himself and Clair. A school psychologist with a scholarly study to back up every one of her opinions, Clair believed that the educational benefits of external rewards were short-lived and that the surest means of instilling a lasting passion for learning lay in letting children discover it on their own. But if given the choice of watching SpongeBob on the couch or doing homework at the kitchen table, Tara would choose the former a hundred times out of a hundred and in time, Wurst feared, she'd become like Patrick, a starfish happiest left beneath his rock on the ocean floor, mesmerized by plankton tumbling past him in the current. But if he restricted Tara to half an hour of TV before bed if, and only if, she received a perfect score on the pretest he administered, then read silently to herself for no less than an hour from one of the children's books he brought home from the public library downtown, the incentive led, at the very least, to a smiley face at the top of her sheet of ruled paper. Clair could argue all she liked about the weaknesses of his approach; it was producing results.

"The five W's," he said. "Who, what, where, when, and why. In a murder case, you're usually given answers to what, where, and when. Who, in most murders, is self evident. When it isn't you have a mystery. Then you have to ask yourself, Why? Who, what, where, when, and why."

He folded the mushrooms he'd pureed in the Cuisinart into onions sautéing on the stove. If he merely chopped them, Tara would pick them out one by one. He had to do the same thing with the ground beef. What made his marinara appealing to Tara, beyond its sugary blandness, was its consistency. Aside from the spaghetti itself, she would be unable to isolate a single ingredient. She was a purist when it came to food, and everything that went into it had to be processed beyond recognition. It was why she liked bologna, Jello, and French fries. Orange juice free of pulp but not oranges themselves, grape juice but not grapes. It was

114

why she liked cheese but preferred cheese spread.

"Should, would, could, before, after, and nothing," he said. "When investigating a murder, there are things you should do and things you would do if only you could. There is a before and an after, and until you can say precisely how they fit together, you have nothing. Should, would, could, before, after, and nothing."

As his marinara simmered, he filled a martini shaker with crushed ice and poured vodka over it. He set an olive stuffed with a pimento into a chilled martini glass, gave the shaker seven stirs, strained the cocktail into his glass. Across the top he floated a drop of dry vermouth. By then the pot of water was boiling, and he cracked spaghetti in half and dropped it in. As it cooked, he quizzed Tara on her spelling of 'through,' 'between,' 'because,' 'around,' 'together,' 'apart,' and 'Warren, Michigan.'

"Warren, Michigan?" he said.

"It's Avril's hometown," Tara replied.

When he was Tara's age, his teacher had been Mrs. Hildebrandt and, as far as he'd known, 'Mrs.' *was* her first name.

"OK," he said, "but is that reason enough to teach second graders to spell it?"

"You have to give Avril a break, Dad," Tara said. "Her fiancé left her, and now all she can talk about is Warren."

"Warren, Michigan huh?" he said. "Whatever. Spell it."

As they ate their suppers and, afterward, Tara read *Witches Don't Do Back Flips*, he thought about Avril

115

Dublonski. At the parent-teacher conference he'd attended with Clair, Avril Dublonski's blondish shoulder-length hair had obscured a tattoo on the back of her neck. He'd sat beside his ex-wife at a thirty-degree angle from Avril at a workstation on two-foot-tall legs, his dress slacked knees pulled to his chest. Avril wore a white skirt and sleeveless blouse, and from the tone of Clair's voice as she interrogated her about each S that should've been an E on Tara's report card he could tell Clair didn't approve of her, which made him like Avril all the more. How Clair could expect their daughter to excel when the only pressure to study at all came from him, he didn't know, but rather than call Clair out on the carpet for it and offer himself up as a human target, he watched Avril's tattoo advance and recede as if through stalks of wheat. He thought at first it was a deer half-hidden by the curvature of her neck, though he could swear that on the front hoof was a slipper and where the head would be a glove.

In the schoolyard as they returned to their cars, Clair said, "Talk about bor-*ing*! It's no wonder Tara isn't in the gifted program. The woman saps energy from intelligent life."

Clair's harsh assessments of others, thrilling to him at the beginning of their marriage, had worn him down over time, and now the mere sound of her voice, gravelly when agitated, worked his nerves. Though when the marriage counselor they'd gone to once their marriage was, in all three opinions, "dead in the water" asked her point-blank if her hypercritical nature wasn't a defense mechanism meant to hide a wellspring of resentment, anger, and insecurity she answered, "Duh," that didn't make it any easier to bear. The closer to retirement he drew, the more certain he was that one's severest criticism ought not to be directed at people at all, no matter how awful the deeds done, but reserved for an ever-evolving, global socio-economic network so vast and intricate it could never be understood in its totality. Every human encounter, from the most innocuous to the most sinister, from the most glorified to the most banal, was both a part of it and determined by it; thus, all one could do was conceive an approximation of it and recognize that one's failures as well as one's accomplishments were no more one's own than a falling leaf's path to the ground was its. The Replacements had understood this as far back as 1983, the year they'd released "Treatment Bound."

"Did you happen to notice," he called to his daughter in the living room, "whether Miss Dublonski is still wearing her engagement ring?"

"Avril?" she replied. "No, she isn't. Now can I watch SpongeBob?"

"Read for another ten minutes," he said, and as she grumbled, he poured the olive at the bottom of his martini glass into his mouth, his mood much improved by the prospect of discovering what Avril Dublonski had tattooed on the back of her neck, a mystery that hitherto hadn't seemed worth investigating.

III

Tara wasn't wearing skinny jeans the day she disap-

117

peared. When Wurst had let her out of his car across the street from her elementary school, she'd been wearing lilac skorts and a white pointelle cardigan, 'skorts' and 'pointelle' words he hadn't even known until he and Claire were asked to provide a description of their daughter for an Amber Alert. They were in the playground, and Claire told the officer interviewing them, "Charlie communicates in generalities, I in specifics. When he says 'purple skirt,' he means 'lilac skorts.' When he says 'sweater,' he means 'pointelle cardigan.'

"I can even remember the clothing lines," she said with the shrill of immanent hysteria. "Will that help? The cardigan was a Bonnie Jean. The skorts were Guess. I bought them at Macy's."

"A purple skirt and white sweater is fine for the officer's purposes," Wurst said.

"In fact," the officer told them, "knowing the clothing lines could prove useful. You know that, Charlie." What he didn't say was . . . in the event that we find her discarded clothes or, worse, have to identify her body . . . for which Wurst was grateful.

A police helicopter circled the school in wider and wider arcs. The sky was smalt, and the finial atop the bell tower cast a needle-thin L upon the four-square courts and whitewashed retaining wall. When the police left, he and Clair sat side-by-side on swings. Before the divorce, they'd brought Tara to the playground many evenings after supper. Going there had been one of her favorite pastimes, and the six-block walk from their small adobe house and back meant an hour he wasn't self-medicating. He could practically see her there in the twilight, playing Duck, Duck, Goose and Honey, Do You Love Me? when he picked her up after school, see her climbing the ropes and jungle gyms. Their motives for having her—to remedy stasis in their marriage and boredom with each other—hadn't been pure, but for the first year of her life her very existence, and the demands it made of them, had taken their minds off their marital difficulties. If a baby was a despot, under its rule kindness was less taxing than spite, and he and Clair might have stayed together, he often thought, if only they'd kept having them. But Clair had been forty when Tara was born, and in the modicum of leisure Tara's toddler-hood granted them demons thought put-to-rest were resurrected. With the regularity of a nervous tic, Clair gave voice again to her fear that he no longer loved her with every fiber of his being, and though he denied it every time, he wondered whether a single fiber remained that cared for her at all.

Then one summer evening on their walk back from the playground Clair said apropos of nothing, "I've consulted a lawyer."

"About what?" he asked.

"Use your powers of deduction," she replied. He was stunned and, weirdly, admiring. He'd thought they were manacled to each other, that freedom from each other was nothing more than the tired premise of a thousand impossible sexual fantasies, and yet once handed to him he was afraid.

"Are you sure?" he asked.

"I could not be surer," she replied.

The sky was smalt and then it wasn't and Wurst could not account for the hours that had passed. He had no recollection of talking to Clair or Clair's leaving him alone on the swings. In his career he'd investigated hundreds of crime scenes, but none had affected him like this. He phoned Clair, asked her how long ago she'd left him in the playground and whether he'd acted strangely in any way.

"You were in shock," she told him. "Do you want me to come back down there?"

"No," he said. "I'm all right. I just have no memory of what happened after we sat down on the swings. Did we talk? Did we make a communication plan? Did we say goodbye to each other?"

"You told me it was all my fault. You kept telling me that Tara's disappearance was all my fault." From the receiver sounded a croak, and then Clair was sobbing with such volume he had to hold the phone at arm's length from his ear. "I don't know, maybe it is my fault," she said between gasps. "I was doing an assessment on a kid, parents totally uncooperative. I kept looking at my watch, trying to let them know I had somewhere to be."

"It isn't your fault," he said. "And it was wrong of me to say it was."

"And the traffic was terrible."

"No one's blaming you."

"If Tara's been taken from us, Charlie, I don't know."

"The East Side Area Command has some of the finest detectives on the force," he said. "You remember Stottermeier, right? We had him and his girlfriend

Kimberly over for dinner. I made duck à l'orange. And Joey Baca? He and his family attended Christ the King back when we did. Maybe they still do."

He knew from experience that his optimism, usually a source of irritation to her, calmed her in times of crisis. "All I'm saying is the department's top brass is on it." It was possible, even likely, he told her, that Tara's kidnapper would attempt to contact her. If he or she did, Clair was to call the private hotline the officer at the crime scene had given her during their interview, then call him immediately thereafter. Though the case hadn't been assigned to him for obvious reasons, he would conduct his own investigation on his own time. "Everything is going to be all right, Clair," he said, though he didn't believe it. "We're going to get our little girl back," he said, though he knew better than most how these things turned out.

The windows into the kindergarten classrooms, plastered with drawings of turkeys made from the outlines of children's hands, caught the headlights of Central Avenue traffic and tossed them onto the asphalt, turf, and sand. Each second that passed diminished the chances of their daughter being found at all, much less alive.

At home he made a vodka martini and picked up after Tara. From her bedroom to the middle of the living room lay a parade of stuffed animals led by the boa constrictor and skunk he'd given to her back when he still carried her around on his chest in a Baby Bjorn. Behind them stood the Snoopies and Woodstocks her grandmother in south Minneapolis had sent her every holiday from Saint Patrick's to Christmas until she died on a winter evening while shoveling her walk, then the snow leopard, Pekinese, elephant, koala bear, penguin, orangutan, frog, condor, crocodile, tiger, antelope, rhinoceros, lamb, opossum, raccoon, weasel, and chimp, each bought for her on a visit to the zoo out of guilt as much as anything. A child of divorced parents, Tara had the spoils to show for it, displayed in separate houses but in matching bedrooms that resembled emporiums, with plumed Mardi Gras masks dangling from her mirror posts and antique wardrobes crammed with clothes she'd worn but once or not at all. That she wanted for nothing and didn't know it couldn't be blamed on her. One of them—which no longer mattered—had given her something that provoked the other to give her something else, and before they knew it they were competing against each other for their daughter's affection. That they were ruining her didn't take Dr. Phil.

Though after one, he phoned Avril Dublonski, figuring he'd leave a Voicemail message for her. When she answered, the gaping static that followed caught him off guard. "Hello?" she said again.

"This is Detective Wurst, Tara Wurst's dad. I apologize for phoning so late."

"It's OK," she said. "I couldn't sleep anyway."

"I won't keep you long."

"I have a sub tomorrow. I can talk to you all night if you like. You're calling about Tara, I take it."

"Yes," he said, "though I'm not officially assigned to the case. I know you gave a witness statement to the detectives who are. Good detectives both." He asked her if she'd noticed anything unusual the day before, nothing that would necessarily stand out in her memory if Tara hadn't gone missing but, now that she had, seemed mildly out of the ordinary, coincidental, or ironic even, in retrospect as if God or fate were making a wry joke.

"A wry joke?" she said.

"Often witnesses fail to provide information pertinent to a case only because they don't see its relevance themselves."

"I understand," she said.

"An offhand remark. An odd expression. Someone behaving slightly out of character. Momentary impressions that would otherwise be forgotten. These sometimes matter."

"There was nothing," she said. "I've scoured the entire day repeatedly, looking for anything that might've signaled what was going to happen, but I keep coming up empty."

"Well," he said, "I'm sorry about your wedding plans. Tara told me they fell through."

"First that, now this. If I didn't know better, I'd say God has a wry sense of humor indeed."

"What happened?" he asked. "Did you see it coming or did it take you by surprise?"

"Both," she said. "When Berto told me he was going back to Poland, I was devastated. But even the devastation, if that's what it was, was like a déjà vu, like something I'd foreseen and even counted upon."

"I know what you mean," he said. "When Tara's

mother—you know Clair—told me she wanted a divorce, it wasn't something I hadn't imagined happening. I had, many times. But that didn't take the sting out of it."

"What about now?" she asked. "This?"

"This?" he said. "My talking to you on the phone at one-thirty in the morning?"

"Uh-huh," she said. "But not just that. Everything. Tara's disappearance. What we're talking about. Berto's breaking up with me. Clair's breaking up with you." Outside a squad car siren sounded. "What's that?" she asked.

"A siren," he replied.

"No," she said. "What you're listening to. I hear music in the background."

He'd turned on the stereo without realizing it, just as he'd made a second and a third vodka martini without realizing it either. "The Replacements," he said.

"Wow," she said. "You like The Replacements."

"Love The Replacements," he said.

"They were from Minneapolis, right?" she said.

"*South* Minneapolis," he said. And then he told her about hearing them live in his high school gym.

4 Time
Shifts

IV

"It was a clown," he tells Rochelle de la Madrid inside the Apothecary, the lounge on the top floor of the Hotel Parq Central, the site of their first date nearly three years ago, "a harlequin."

He is married to Avril Dublonski now and has been happily so for over a year.

124

But for three weeks, ever since the arrest of The Skinny Jeans Killer, a.k.a. Lucas ("Freebird") Mahoney-Villa, thanks to what Police Chief Claudia Estovan-Clark called his "superb detective work," which overnight made him irresistible to Rochelle, he has been having an affair with her, and now he isn't sure if his marriage is happy or not. Rochelle believes that were it not for him, Mahoney-Villa would still be at-large, preying upon women in jeggings, though in truth once Mahoney-Villa was dubbed The Skinny Jeans Killer, most of the women living in the city stopped wearing them, which allowed Homicide, with help from the FBI, to lure Mahoney-Villa into custody with a decoy.

"I don't know what I was hoping for. A mandala? A lotus? A cosmic egg? But a fool? A jester? When I finally ascertained what my child's second grade teacher had tattooed on her neck, by then I'd asked her to marry me. You laugh, but by then half the calendars in Warren, Michigan had our wedding date written on them. I proposed to Avril on a Sunday afternoon and by Monday evening the elder Dublonskis had the Knights of Columbus lodge on Ryan Road booked for the reception and her sister Maeve had set up a website with a ticker counting off the days, hours, minutes, seconds, and nanoseconds left until our exchange of vows at Saint Sylvester's."

Tara has been missing for over two years. Some nights he watches SpongeBob SquarePants in the living room while Avril prepares her next day's lessons in the kitchen. Afterward she'll ask him if he remembers anything that happened in any episode and he won't, not one moment or line. It's as if he's returned from the other side of the television screen, from a fully animated underwater world where he is conducting an investigation on his own time, interviewing SpongeBob, his pet snail Gary, his boss Eugene Krabs, his friends Patrick and Sandy, his arch nemesis Squidward. Though each claims no knowledge of his daughter's whereabouts, he suspects they are protecting her and as soon as he returns to his home where Avril sips chamomile tea while checking the status updates of her Facebook friends, Tara will emerge from beneath a rock in Bikini Bottoms and eat Krabby Patties at the Krusty Krab. Avril wants a baby, and on the three or four nights a week when he isn't working undercover, he tries to impregnate her. On the nights he is, he leaves that other Wurst behind, and because Avril is so trusting he imagines that the Wurst putting murderers behind bars or, as is the case tonight, about to retire to a fully comped suite with de la Madrid is no more real than the Wurst who dreams of interrogating Sheldon Plankton at the Chum Bucket.

Rochelle sets down her Twelve-Mile Limit, a prohibition era cocktail made with rum, whiskey, and brandy, on an art deco bev-nap. "Clowns are creepy. If I found a clown on someone I was sleeping with, it might take more than a set wedding date to keep me with him. It might take a set appointment with a tattoo-removal specialist."

"I don't mind it," he says. "Though if I'd been able to see the damn thing at the parent-teacher conference that morning, I wonder if it would have possessed me like it did. As it was, I couldn't take my mind off it. For weeks I imagined pulling back Avril's hair and seeing what? I didn't know. But you know what? Every time I was with her and could've asked her point-blank to see it, I forgot all about it. The tattoo never crossed my mind."

He's fifty-two, she's thirty-one, and if the French calculation is to be trusted, they are the perfect ages for each other now. But if his second wife presents an obstacle to their ever being more than secret lovers, so too does de la Madrid's fiancé, Carlos Santillanes, the oldest son of a family that prides itself in a lineage dating back to a conquistador born in León in 1542. According to Rochelle, she is in "like" with Carlos, but will marry him anyway within the year because of the endorsement their union has received from all four parents, which, she believes, is more important to a successful marriage than passion or even love. What she has with him, Wurst, she refuses to quantify, and why should she? She likes him well enough to go to bed with him. And yet he can't help thinking that their timing was off, that if she'd only found him attractive enough to bed *before* the apprehension of Mahoney-Villa, they could've made their relationship public, gotten engaged, wed. Though of German ancestry traceable back to a great grandfather who in 1900 worked as a foreman in a Neenah, Wisconsin foundry, he could've won her parents over. Probably. Maybe.

"What's funny is Avril can't stand it. Hates it in fact. She and an ex-boyfriend dared each other to get tattoos, the stipulations being one, that each would choose the tattoo the other would receive and two, neither could see the tattoo until it was done."

"So she winds up with a clown on the back of her neck," Rochelle says.

"And he winds up with the head of a palomino on his left ass cheek."

"She was smart to choose the back of her neck," Rochelle says.

"I guess."

"I think it's sweet," Rochelle says, which surprises him. She wets her teeth with her tongue and grins at him. "I bet you would've agreed to the same thing if I'd dared you."

"But you didn't dare me," he says. "You wouldn't even go out with me after our second date. And all because of that mild faux pas of mine. I've regretted it ever since, I'll have you know."

"What faux pas?"

"What I said about Clair that day. On our drive back from the rodeo. You know, about wishing her dead. You lost interest in me after that. Don't deny it."

"I didn't lose interest in you because of that," she says. "My God, you had a child, Charlie."

So that was it. He had a child.

"Open mouth," she says. "Insert foot."

He had a child, and now he doesn't.

In their suite they undress and embrace. Standing beside the bed, he in boxer shorts, she in just her jewelry, he slides three fingers between her legs and parts her labia with the middle one. Skinny jeans are now passé. But if the year in which they were the rage

128

seems like eons ago, The Replacements performing in his high school gym might as well have occurred in a past life, and as he and Rochelle kiss it's as if he's become a cartoon version of himself, folded into a future in which he is of the world but hardly in it at all.

Huntsville Rodeo, 1968

3rd Young Boy – No Name

The boy's father followed two winding ruts through Texas prairie in which snakes flourished, the boy was certain. His father wasn't driving fast, and the boy felt calm smelling the cigarettes his father smoked and listening to the staticky broadcasts of country music from the radio station in Killeen. The Jeep was roofless, and the sun at eleven o'clock warmed the backs of his arms and neck as he strained against the seatbelt to see beyond the hinged curves of dark metal where a door had been. The boy bet against himself as each parched spot disappeared behind him that on the next would be a rattlesnake, coral snake, or copperhead. Venomous varieties intrigued him most, but he would be happy to see a king snake or even a bull snake.

But he saw no snakes, and soon the brush gave way to cottonwood trees, and he and his father were waved through a checkpoint by two MPs in combat dress. The men saluted his father, and his father saluted back, and the boy felt proud that his father trusted him enough to take him into a restricted zone. The boy was used to checkpoints —when returning to the base, the car he rode in was always stopped—but this was the first through which he'd passed that led even deeper into the base and, as the canopy above him grew dense with foliage, he experienced a deep thrill at being taken to a place he wouldn't entirely understand.

The road ended at a collection of bamboo huts, the

130

thatched roofs sloped like tiers of switch brooms, the air laden with insects and dust. Above the boy, nets and high tension wires supported vines that blotted out all but peek holes of sky. "Everything in eyesight was brought over from Vietnam for the purpose of simulating combat conditions overseas," his father explained. "It might look like an amusement park, but it isn't. The whole place is booby-trapped and dangerous, all twenty acres of it. Deep pits you can't see because they're covered with layers of mud and straw. Trip wires. Rope snares."

His father put out a cigarette in the ashtray, then turned off the dashboard radio, his hand, darkly haired and tanned, truncated at the wrist by a starched camel cuff. "Stay beside me and nothing bad will happen to you, understand?"

The boy nodded and climbed out of the Jeep. Inside the compound, the air was shadowy and cool. A door hung open on one of the huts, and through the filtered light the boy saw a grass mat, table, and large wooden bowl filled with rice. From another door hung an oxbow, worn smooth, and cattle bells, tarnished and blue. Neither people nor animals occupied the compound, but from the sureness of his father's pace the boy assumed he knew the precise location of each hazard. They passed a livestock pen, cistern, and bamboo hut larger than any of the others; through the entrance the boy could see wooden pews and an altar made of weathered boards over which a chipped white cross hung. Beyond the chapel lay a still larger hut, a medical insigne strung between bamboo poles, and the boy followed his father inside to where a dozen army cots led to an examination table, standing cabinets, refrigerator, sink.

His father flipped a switch and overhead lights lit the infirmary. "Why don't you lie on a cot," his father said. "I have inventory to finish for Monday's maneuvers. Can I trust you to stay on the cot?"

The boy sat down on threadbare canvas stretched across a metal frame.

"It'll take me all of twenty minutes. Then we're off to the rodeo. I promise."

The boy pulled his legs up onto the cot and listened to vials tinkling against one another. His father was a doctor, and the boy could remember a time before the draft when his father went to work each morning at a clinic in Milwaukee. He couldn't remember much about Milwaukee aside from a park where he and his mother walked, and a pond that froze over in the winter except for where a spring bubbled up in the center, and the geese that encircled the spring, squawking and nipping at each other on the ice, but he remembered the clinic, the antiseptic smell of it, and he didn't mind lying on a cot in a place where the smell was the same.

His mother left because the government couldn't make up its mind whether to send his father to Vietnam or not. This his father had explained to him, and the boy could not think of a reason to doubt him; one day his father came home from Darnall Army Hospital with orders to report to Dau Tieng; two weeks later new orders stated that he was to continue treating army personnel at Fort Hood. Two months after that he was ordered to Chu Lai; five days passed, and he was ordered to remain on base. When his father was called up a third time, his mother broke every piece of dinnerware, china, and crystal they owned. The boy had watched her lift each plate, cup, glass, and goblet over her head and splinter it on the kitchen floor of the duplex the army had issued to them. Again the government retracted its orders, but by then she had gone to live with her own mother in a trailer park in southern California, and now when he tried to picture her face, he couldn't.

"It's nice we're having this day together," his father called to him. "Soon you'll be grown up, and I'll wonder why we didn't have more of them."

The boy turned onto his side and stared out the doorway at the bamboo huts. If the village had been replicated to simulate combat conditions overseas, perhaps the government had introduced snakes indigenous to region. The boy considered that two of the most important snakes in the world—the reticulated python and krait—were native to Vietnam, and he sat up on the cot. If he waited long enough, perhaps he would see one moving through the straw and mud outside.

He asked his father if he could wait for him on the stoop outdoors, and his father lowered his clipboard. "Wander off, and I swear to God you'll wish you hadn't."

The boy knew nurses found his father attractive, and he thought his father could remarry in a second if he wanted to. In the meantime, Mrs. Temple cleaned their house and fixed his meals, or he went next door to the Halls, a Mormon family whose five boys included him in games of kickball and tag, and these arrangements suited him. When his mother had been gone a month, his father told him he was going to start dating again. He said that if he ever brought a nurse home, the boy should treat her politely, but that he should not, however motherly she acted toward him, confuse her with his actual mother who, if she returned, should never hear of these exploits. *Exploits* was the word his father had used, and because of the nasty sound of it, the boy had cried. He still didn't know what the word meant, but he wished he hadn't cried. Since then his father had introduced him to three nurses, and though the boy would have liked to tell his father that he preferred each to his mother, he sensed his tears had put the subject off-limits.

From the stoop, he looked at the path he and his father had taken. Surely if he stayed on it, no harm would come to him, and with a greater vantage he believed his chances of seeing a snake would improve. He walked slowly, placing each boot in the larger print his father had left, but checking nonetheless for trip wires and odd marks in the straw and mud that might signal pits or snares. He saw no wires or marks, but when he came to the cistern he turned around and looked back at the chapel. If ever there was a place for a snake, it was there, he thought, and imagined reticulated pythons coiled on the altar, thousands of kraits slithering between the pews. He stepped toward the entrance cautiously, testing the ground with his boot heel before applying his full weight. A few feet short of the doorway, he stopped. When his father saw that he'd wandered off, he'd be in deep trouble. This he knew, and yet he thought it unfair: explain all he might, his father would never understand the power snakes had over him, how he dreamed of them in his sleep and the sight of even a garter snake moving in a continuous series of S's across a lawn lodged in his brain, making him forget to wash his hands before a meal or brush his teeth after eating.

When the boy heard his father exclaim, "Don't tell me. Don't *even* tell me," he darted into the cool half-light of the sanctuary.

His parents had been of two minds about corporal punishment, but once his mother had left there had been no one to protect him from his father's hand, and as he sat on a pew, he readied himself for the humiliation of being spanked—the knuckles against his belly as his father's finger's manipulated the small zipper, the rush of air against his privates as his trousers were yanked to his shins, and the bony hardness of his father's knee as his body was folded in half across it. Each time it came, the smarting his father's palm inflicted stunned him. One couldn't prepare for it, and yet he preferred being spanked to his parents' arguments about whether or not to.

The boy sniffed the air for his father's scent, cowered in expectation of his father's hands. When neither came, he stepped back outside to find his father slung upside-down from a tree, his pendulous body clenched at the ankle by a rope snare. On the ground below his father, his father's billfold, keys, lighter, penknife, ciga-

135

rettes, change. "I thought I told you not to wander off," he said.

"I'm sorry," the boy replied.

Two blood vessels formed a V across his father's forehead, and his father's eyes bulged in their sockets. The point of his father's tie, the same camel as his shirt and slacks, was flipped over the clip. It was strange to see the crown of his father's head, the wiry stubble that covered his scalp. Not even when his father was angry did his face so bloat and puff.

"Do you think you could put your snake cards away?" his father asked. "Do you think you could do that?"

The boy hadn't realized he still held the cards, smelling of the bubble gum they came with, and returned them to his pants pocket.

"What am I going to do with you?" his father said. "You're seven years old, and you think you have the whole world figured out. Well, I'm thirty-two, and what I've figured out I could fit on a postage stamp."

"What could've happened to me?" the boy asked.

His father's eyes widened. "Look at me," he said. "This could be you,"

Not all of his father's Pall Malls had fallen to the ground because his father found one in the pack in his breast pocket and put it to his mouth. "How about a light?" he said through pinched lips, and the boy picked up the lighter from the ground, pulled back the shiny silver cap, and flicked the flint wheel. A flame, blue at its fuel source, burst from his fist.

"Well done," his father said. "Now hold it up here

like a good boy. High. That's right."

The boy stood on his tiptoes, his thumb on the gas lever, and followed the flame past his father's eyebrows and nose to the bright orange bead it made at the end of the cigarette.

"Good," his father said. "Thanks."

Smoke left his nostrils as if from a chimney, churned before his Adam's apple, shirt collar, and colorful bands of service decorations.

"I'd hoped bringing you here would help us establish trust. You're getting to be too old for spankings. I don't want to give them to you anymore. But it's time you listened to your old man and trusted me when I tell you things."

The boy examined the creases in his father's slacks, how they rose from his cinched belt and brass buckle and made a pair of crumpled cups at his field boots.

"Now I know that in a chapel you feel safe. At peace. Even if it's made of sticks and a strong wind could level it. But, you see, the enemy knows this. They know that when an American soldier enters a recognizable place of worship, he's liable to relax a little, let down his guard, put his foot down where he shouldn't. And the army knows that the enemy knows this. That's why when it rebuilt this village, it made damn sure it booby-trapped the sanctuary."

His father gently rotated as he spoke, and the boy admired how sturdily his father's starched shirt fell from his narrow trunk to his wide shoulders. His father had boxed as a youth, and the boy could only imagine how it would be to have such a build, to occupy such a form, to be a presence that, depending on the situation, instilled fear or inspired confidence.

"Well, I might as well let you in on the good news. I spoke to your mother last week, and she's decided to come back to us. I pick her up at the airport on Tuesday."

The boy supposed he should feel happy about this.

"Hey," his father said, "why so glum?"

"Why are you so glum," asked the boy.

His father's face was graver than he'd ever seen it. Then he realized that his father was smiling. "For me, it's not that simple, son. Now I know your mother loves you, and I have every reason to believe she loves me, too, but a month after she left I thought she was gone for good. Now I have to put an end to a relationship your mother must never hear about, you understand me?"

"With Monette, Trudy, or Jill?" the boy asked.

"With Monette," his father said and let his tarstained filter fall to the ground. "She's coming along with us to the rodeo. I tried to talk her out of it, but her heart's set on it. Now I haven't told her about your mother's coming back to roost, but I suppose I'll have to today."

His father grabbed hold of the rope that held his ankle, slipped his boot from the noose, and dropped onto his feet.

"If this were Nam," he said as he collected his effects, "we'd be in a real bind."

•

The boy liked Monette. Big-boned, she laughed easily, and when one morning she'd gotten down on the floor with him to construct skyscrapers with his erector set, she seemed to care less if his mother's robe exposed cross-sections of breasts flushed and powdered after showering. His father left the government Jeep in the lot behind the commissary, and they drove off base in the two-year-old Chrysler station wagon his father had bought, after his induction, for the family to make the move from Wisconsin to Texas. Outside Fort Hood lay the city of Killeen, and the boy watched familiar landmarks pass by in the glare—Walker's Shoe Store, Big Boy, the Plaza Cinema—before his father stopped beside the curb outside The Hidalgos, a terra cotta apartment complex with verandas overlooking a fenced-in swimming pool, the blue of which gleamed through green cedar slats.

His father took the duffel bag of civvies lying between them on the seat and told him to wait in the car. "We'll be here before you can say Jack Frost." He winked as he closed the driver's side door, then walked toward the entrance to the apartments with a swagger the boy associated with weekends, when his father was granted leave.

Across the street, the temperature displayed outside Cattleman's Bank & Trust read ninety-nine degrees. When the boy looked again, it read one hundred, and the air inside the Chrysler was sweltering. The key was in the ignition, and the boy felt reasonably sure turning it would start the air-conditioning, but he didn't know whether a foot on the brake was needed to keep the station wagon from lurching into the silver Corvette parked in front of it. The windows were electric, so there was no way to lower them, and if his father came from the complex and saw a car door open, he'd conclude that he'd caught the boy in the process of wandering off, and the trust they'd found would be lost.

Sweat trickled down his spine into the undersides of his canvas shorts. When he scooted onto a dry part of the seat, the Naugahyde seared his thighs, and he replanted himself in the warm puddles of his own liquid. "Come on, Dad," he said.

He tried to predict when minutes would change on the bank's digital display, counted to a hundred eighteen times, then stared longingly at the slender strips of blue visible through the fence. A bikini-clad woman got up from her chaise lounge, crossed to the edge of the pool, tested the water with her toes, and dove in. Then she climbed out, walked back to her spot on the grass, and dried off with a beach towel. The entire action, through the fence slats, was like it had been caught on super eight.

"Damn it, Dad," he said. "What the hell's keeping you."

No sooner had the cuss words left his mouth than his father and Monette came from the building, and the boy ran to them, hoping to air dry his clothes and give the moisture on the seat a chance to evaporate before Monette sat down on it. "Atta boy," his father said, drawing him to his side and patting his shoulder. Inside, his father had shed his officer's khakis in favor of blue jeans and a western shirt with pearl buttons.

"Why, look at you," said Monette. "You're white as a ghost." She knelt before him on the sidewalk, tugged up on his pants and down on his shirt, freeing fabric from his skin as his father ambled toward the Chrysler. "That father of yours. Leaving you with the windows rolled up. It's a wonder you didn't turn to soda pop." She laughed, her tanned face as refreshing to behold as iced tea. She wore a white sundress, white button earrings, matching white cowboy boots, cowboy hat, and purse, and as the boy saw how her spaghetti straps traversed the ridges of her wide clavicles and disappeared in coppery cascades of curls, he hoped he'd be able to preserve her memory better than he had his mother's.

"Come on," she said, grasping his hand. "We don't want to miss the rodeo."

His father had the station wagon running. The boy opened the passenger door for Monette and was met by a cool burst of air-conditioned air. His perspiration, he was glad to see, had vanished from the seat entirely. "Why don't you sit in the back," his father said, and Monette said, "Oh, let him sit up front with the big people," and the boy moved over next to his father.

Soon they were traveling through farmland scored by creeks and forested ravines too quickly for the boy to worry about missing a snake. They were out there, he imagined, seventy-five to a hundred per acre, basking in the July heat, and it comforted him to think, as thousands of acres arched out on either side of him, that the snake would fare better than humans in the event of a war like the one overseas. In these parts they outnumbered people and lived in underground lairs where even napalm could not reach them.

The boy liked being sandwiched between Monette and his father. Monette smelled of cocoa butter, his father of the Avon cologne his mother gave him every Christmas, and as Monette engaged his father in conversations about people the boy didn't know, movies the boy hadn't seen, and the presidential race between Humphrey and Nixon, she said more than she needed to in order to keep him involved and interested. When he went with his parents on outings, they rarely spoke to each other, but when they did his mother spelled words she didn't want him to hear, and though he appreciated Monette's efforts to include him, a fear gathered within him that sooner or later his father would tell her the news. Anne's very fragile, the boy imagined him saying. That's why she mustn't learn about us, you understand? Then it occurred to the boy that perhaps his father had already told her, that in the privacy of her apartment he'd explained to her how his mother was liable to wreck the TV and hi-fi when she finished splintering all the replaced dishes.

The fifty cent lots maintained by the Texas Department of Corrections filled to capacity, his father parked on the tire-rutted lawn of a dilapidated bungalow five blocks from the prison and paid the owner, an elderly lady whose pink and brown muumuu fell to sore-inflicted calves, a dollar for the honor. "Now you folks run along and enjoy the rodeo, y'hear?" she said, stuffing the bill into her knee-high nylons as she fanned herself with a newspaper. "I'm just going to sit here in the shade of this old parasol tree until all the steer-roping and bronco-riding's over for another year, and mind no one makes off with your fancy wheels."

His father took off his cowboy hat. "We're much obliged," he said.

As the three strolled toward the grandstand and gates, the boy admired the ease with which his father led them through the fracas. Banners, strung across the street, announced the dates of the annual rodeo, and along the sidewalk skirting the prison's twelve foot-high chain-linked fence, veterans' organizations and church groups vended Styrofoam plates piled high with barbecued ribs, chicken fried steak, grilled pork chops. Between them, tables displayed firearms that predated Texas' statehood, common knots, odd variet-ies of barbed wire.

On one table stood cowboy hats of woven straw, stacked by size. "Let's buy a hat for the little man," Monette said, "before the sun bakes his scalp to a crackily crisp."

"What do you know?" his father exclaimed. "You're getting a hat." And ground his knuckles into the boy's head.

Soon Monette and his father were having a grand time placing hats on him, large ones that covered his face, brims resting flat on his shoulders, and small ones he balanced as if they were teacups. But he didn't mind. With each, he withdrew and fired an imaginary six-shooter, making them laugh.

"Billy the Kid," said his father.

"Liberty Valance," said Monette, and kissed the boy's nose.

Then, as his father placed on his head a hat that fit, the boy spotted the traveling rattlesnake show. It had been set up across the street, in a red brick building with plate glass windows advertising seed and machinery parts. Above the doorway, a handmade sign: MORE ANGRY RATTLESNAKES IN ONE PLACE THAN MOST PEOPLE WILL SEE IN THEIR LIFE-TIMES! Below it, a second sign: ADMISSION 75¢. The boy made a beeline for it, then stood mesmerized before the smoky interior and the beige shadows of spectators within. Outside an adjacent building —a firehouse, its red great doors hitched back—cowboys in aprons grilled rattlesnake over an open flame and served it with biscuits and gravy to customers amassed on the pavement. Monette gathered him in her arms, her curls sprung and sagging after chasing him through the throngs.

"Like to go inside and see the snakes?" she asked.

"I would," the boy replied.

"Maybe we can after the rodeo. I'll talk to your dad. He seems to be in a giving mood."

His father was waiting for them at the turnstile, smoking a Pall Mall. "Remember what I said about wandering off? About how I was done spanking you? How from here on out we were relying on trust?"

"Yes," said the boy.

"Good," his father said. "I thought maybe you'd forgotten."

Inside the gate they were frisked perfunctorily by armed guards who let them pass, and sat down on a bleacher halfway between the press boxes and rodeo yard, the boy on one side of his father, Monette on the other. Below, three inmates dressed as clowns took turns provoking a bull by sweeping matadors' capes in front of it, tumbling at the last second out of the path of its lowered horns. Stilted guard towers rose from the stadium's four corners, and in the lookouts stood sharpshooters, their high-powered rifles aimed at the turf.

Concessionaires roamed the aisles, shouting out their provisions. His father handed the boy a dollar from his wallet. "This is for Pronto Pups, Nehi, whatever you like."

The boy thanked him, stuffed the money into his pants pocket next to the snake cards as his father hollered, "Beer! We need a couple of beers over here!" His father handed a dollar to Monette, who passed it to an enormous man in a black suit and bolo tie sitting on her left. Beyond the big man sat his waif of a wife, and between that woman and the bearded concessionaire, who nipped the caps off two Hamms and poured them at once into plastic cups, sat six children, a track of sunburned thighs over which the floppy green bill traveled hand to hand. As the enormous man gave them their beers, he told them he was a Baptist minister stationed in a small west Texas parish and explained that he'd brought his wife and children to the rodeo to help him pray for his brother, an inmate competing as a bronco rider.

"I'm not saying what he did was right," the minister said. "Fraud's a crime, but he and I grew up in Cleveland, and I can tell you that before today he hadn't come any closer to breaking in a wild mustang than you or I."

"What's he doing riding one then?" Monette asked as the man took off his jacket and folded it on his lap.

"Same as the others, vying for conjugal visits, movie and library passes, steak and lobster dinners. It's nothing short of institutionalized barbarism, you ask me. Look around you. Everyone's thinking they're so civilized and superior. But I ask you, if they're so civilized, why don't they bring a real rodeo to town? A rodeo with rated cowboys? Men who've spent their lives roping steers and taming broncos? I'll tell you why. Because people here have no interest in seeing anything but society's most ostracized and loathed of men bucked onto their heads or impaled on a bull's horns. It's enough to break a man's faith, is what it is."

As they watched the steer roping and then the calf roping, the boy thought the minister was right. When an inmate failed to loop heels with his lasso, the audience slapped their thighs, laughed and pointed. When an inmate managed to succeed, he bungled the takedown or the tying of hooves, giving people another opportunity to jeer. Still, as the sun dropped behind the grandstand, and the shadow of the prison, with its smokestacks and sentinels, advanced across trampled clods of earth, the boy was glad to be spending the afternoon with his father and Monette. His father might as easily have asked Mrs. Temple to baby-sit him.

On his fifth beer his father looked past Monette and said to the minister, "How would you like to look after my son for twenty minutes? He's a good boy. He won't be a problem. It's just that my lady friend and I have matters we need to discuss in private."

"Why, it'd be an honor," said the minister. "He's a well-behaved boy, I can tell by looking at him."

"Matters?" Monette said. "What matters is it's starting to get chilly. Now be a gentleman and put your arm around me."

"I have something to talk to you about," his father said.

Monette laughed. "We talk all the time. Finally we go somewhere as a family and you have to ask a total stranger to look after the boy." She reached across his father's lap, placed her hand on the boy's knee as she glanced back at the minister. "Don't take it personally, padre. I'm sure you're a perfectly trustworthy guardian."

The boy's father returned Monette's hand to her lap. "Now let's get one thing straight, OK?" he said. "We never have been, nor ever will be, a family."

The boy looked past his father at Monette, saw her plastic cup trembling in her sun-tanned fingers.

"I know we're not a family *yet*," she said. "Now give me a kiss."

His father squeezed his knee as he whispered something in Monette's ear, and the boy's stomach fell as if her were careering on a roller coaster. A moment passed, and Monette said, "So that's what you wanted to tell me? Why couldn't you have told me three hours ago, when we were *you-know-what*, all gaga?"

"Monette," said the boy's father.

"Don't Monette me," she replied.

"The woman saved me," his father said. "If not for her, I'd be overseas right now, you can bet on that."

"If not for her what?" Monette said. "Breakdowns? Of all the schemes I've heard of."

"Hey, I didn't get us into this unconscionable war," his father said.

Below, inmates in their black-and-whites cleared the rodeo yard for bronco riding. When the boy looked at Monette again, she was making her way to the aisle, stepping over the legs of the minister's children, sloshing beer onto the cowboy hats of people sitting on the next bleacher down.

"Oh, for Christ's sake," his father said and rose, sighing, to his boots. "Watch my son, will you?" he said to the minister. "Please don't let him wander off."

His father caught up with Monette scrambling down the risers, and over two sections of spectators the boy saw his father's jaw tighten as she jerked her wrist free of him. They exchanged words, Monette turned to walk away, and his father yanked her by the elbow in a half circle.

At the far end of the rodeo yard, a bronco reared from an open gate, catapulting an inmate headlong over its mane. When the boy tried to locate his father and Monette again, they were gone, and in their place a concessionaire squeezed ketchup and mustard onto a hotdog. "Why don't you sit over here next to me?" the minister said, and the boy moved down next to him and watched as one rider after another was bucked from his horse. "The idea is to stay in the saddle for the full count," the minister explained. "A rider who can do that can pretty much lead a bronco to the stables, because he's broken the creature, and the creature respects him. But I wouldn't set my hopes too high. Most of the riders you're seeing today aren't capable of commanding respect from man or beast."

When the time came for his brother to ride, the minister said, "Would you help us pray for Jimmy? You think you can do that? I'm afraid the poor soul's going to need all the help he can get."

The boy imagined the minister's brother staying on his horse until it stopped bucking. None of the other riders had been able to do it, and the boy hoped the minister's brother would be the first, but no sooner had the horse reared from the gate than the rider was hurled sideways from his saddle onto the dirt. The horse spun on its hind legs and, as the minister's brother rose to his haunches, its forelegs buckled and the points of its shoulders drove his head into the earth. In an instant the horse righted itself and trotted across the rodeo yard with lazy pasterns. Where it had fallen, Jimmy lay motionless, his face and upper body pressed into the earth, his legs sticking out as if from a manhole.

"Good God," said the minister, wiping perspiration from his forehead with a handkerchief. "I have to go down there. They have to let me see my brother." The minister's shoulders heaved as he hobbled past his wife and children, and the boy, following in his wake, waited patiently for him to take each step down the narrow walkway. When the minister started down the second set of risers, steps that led to the rodeo yard and the electrified fence surrounding it, the boy turned and walked toward the exit. He passed the guard who had frisked him, the turnstile in front of which his father had waited on Monette and him, and walked up the street to the rattlesnake show. The crowds had thinned, but the cowboys in aprons were still grilling snake for those who desired it, and outside the seed and machinery parts store he handed the dollar his father had given him to a man who looked old enough to have defended the Alamo.

"Some people think there's nothing more treacherous than a rattlesnake," the old man said, his hat brim pulled low across his brow and his shirt sleeves rolled up to the tops of his arms, the blood vessels of which lay on the surface of his skin like unearthed water mains, "but I prefer to think of the rattlesnake as the 'gentleman snake' on account of the warning it always gives its victims. Once inside, I hope to show you that a rattlesnake's no different than any other creature, doing what it must to get by, putting to use the gifts God gave it. You frighten easy?"

The boy shrugged, and the old man handed him his change. "Well, come along then," he said.

The boy followed the old man inside and waited while he set up a stepladder beside a large wooden pen. Then the boy climbed to the top and peered down over rough-hewn lumber at so many snakes he could not make out one complete body in the entangled, writhing mass. In his pocket were the snake cards, and he thought how he would never have to look at them again after this. The old man ascended steps behind the pen, then lowered himself into the pen and waded through the snakes over to the boy.

"Been bit so many times the venom's stopped affecting me," the old man said. "Or maybe I've just been around them so long they consider me one of their own. Whichever the case, they hardly ever strike me anymore, but when they do, I might sleep poorly for a night or two, but that's about the extent of it."

The old man picked up a snake and pinched open its mouth, opaque roof and pink, translucent fangs. In the boy's mind his father hung upside down above the pit, gently rotating.

What would become of him, he wondered. What would become of any of them?

Tina Louise

voice

My wife Geena comes home from her job at the health food store and tells me she's been promoted to Health & Beauty Aids Manager. I find this ridiculous, as she is 5'4", 190 pounds, and unhealthy. But I tell her, "That's great, honey. I couldn't be happier for you." We're in the kitchenette where I'm feeding organic formula I've warmed on the stovetop to our three-month-old, Tina Louise, whom we named after the actress who played Ginger on the popular syndicated television series.

Geena's excitement is evident, and she asks me if I know what this means, her promotion. I whisper, "I do," not wanting to wake up the neighbors whose nightly harangues can set off Tina Louise's bawling. It's after midnight, and the complex we live in has quieted down, the Hendersons to the east and the Weavers to the west having ceased their bellyaching at long last. Even the two fraternal brothers in the apartment above ours have put away their barbecue tongs and boom-box, closed their cooler, and gone looking for women instead of whistling at them from their balcony at the streetwalkers below. "It'll mean greater equity for us," I say, "mean we can pay back a little more on our credit card debts, mean we can put aside a little more for Tina Louise's college education and maybe one day move from this rats' nest into a place of our own."

My contempt for A-One Apartments—from its wafer-thin walls to its bargain basement fixtures—is due in no small measure to the dangers it will present out daughter when she begins to explore the world on hands and knees and feet: the toxic flakes of yellow paint she might strip from the window sills; the missing struts in the cast iron railing she might crawl through; and the swimming pool, as hazardous filled as drained, no lifeguard ever on duty. Geena sets a freezer bag on the countertop. I say, "So you feeling worse than usual."

"Let me ask you something, Hank. How often have you heard me complain about these?" She says this in the same exasperated voice she uses with underlings, then displays the backs of her hands as if they've been chosen for careers in advertising.

"Often," I admit. "But I don't want to argue with you, honey."

"I don't want to argue with you either," she says. "But I'd like to know if you ever really listen to me, if you're even capable of it."

Her eyebrows rise, and I know I'm beaten. In the department she's leaving, the Deli, her hands were exposed to industrial cleansers, high-speed rotary blades, juices pressed from onions, garlic, and wheatgrass. In the department she'll manage she'll have access to natural remedies and dietary supplements, to marshmallow root for whooping cough and colloidal silver for mumps, to tea tree oil for ringworm and wild lettuce extract for sleeplessness, and many other products that will come in handy as we face the onslaught of childhood maladies.

"Honey, I'm pretty sure I've heard you complaining about the skin on your hands flaking, scabbing, and

153

smelling of vegetables. But with all those sample packets you'll be bringing home, those nagging problems will soon be ancient history."

"Ha!" she says.

"What do you mean, 'Ha'?" I say.

"I've never complained about my hands. My hands are perfect. They belong in commercials. It's my nails. In the deli they were always cracking."

She presses her fingertips together against the flats of her palms so I can see how cracked her nails are, how wracked the cuticles, how blotched the finish. I remove the bottle from our baby's mouth and daub spittle from her chin with a hand-cloth laundered in an eco-friendly fabric softener. In three hours I'm due at the unloading dock of Tender Loving Care Bakery, my truck gassed and loaded for a route that will take me from Albuquerque to Los Alamos, where successors of the physicists who developed the bomb await their loaves of Bavarian rye and stone-ground wheat, baguettes laced with gruyere and dinner rolls sprinkled with parmesan.

"I'm glad you'll be able to wear your nails long, honey," I say.

In truth I'm happy for her. I offer her a halfhearted smile, the best I can summon at this hour of the night, and sit down at our kitchen table as Geena removes a half-gallon tub of praline-caramel-twirl ice milk from its bag and Frisbees the lid into the trash. Across the table from me she sits down, spoon in hand and ice milk cradled like a tom-tom.

"I am going to wear them long, Hank," she says.

"I'm going to wear them so long they'll look like Tina Louise Number One's claws.

Tina Louise Number One is not the human baby we so cherish, but the thirteen-inch desert iguana we purchased together a year and a half earlier at Cold Blooded Creatures in the mall, before we were married or even knew each other. Geena had come to the shop for the purpose of buying the reptile, but when she got there she found its price had risen a hundred dollars and she could no longer afford it. I'd come to the shop hoping only to leave with a pet, thinking that caring for it would take my mind off heroin. From the newt and skink aisle, I listened to her argue with a stoned high school kid who told her he'd lose his job if he sold her the iguana at the price she wanted. In the display window, a three-foot alligator named Mickey languished in a plastic swimming pool of brackish scum.

As Geena stared down at it, I introduced myself to her, explained that I'd overheard her conversation with the clerk and believed that God had placed me in the shop to be of service.

"What do you mean," she replied, "by service?"

"If you'll let me buy you lunch," I said, "I'll explain."

She eyed me cautiously. "I'm probably the world's biggest fool," she said, "but okay. Okay. I'll let you buy me lunch."

We went next door to an espresso bar where we ordered free trade coffees and organic veggie wraps and sat down before a plate glass storefront through which the sunlight fell, lighting up the flavored syrups that

155

crenelated the bar. "Here I am," she said. "Tell me how you can help."

I took a deep breath and told her that I'd been a heroin addict for the better part of my adult life. I was thirty-five when I quit, and I told her how, for eleven years, heroin had been the staple of my existence. I told her as well how I'd supported my habit by calculating odds at racetracks and selling my blue sheets for fifteen dollars each at Belmont, Pimlico, and Churchill Downs, and how one year I picked all three winners of the Triple Crown and made three hundred thousand dollars. I told her how a talent that had never failed me failed me at Ruidosa Downs, in southeastern New Mexico, how I managed to squander my last hundred on heroin in the Apache town of Mescalero, and how, bereft and bankrupt, I wrestled with my hunger on White Sands Missile Base, wishing for a test explosion to obliterate me from my addiction once and for all. When none came, I slowly regained my senses and vowed to free myself from every vestige of my former life, from my love for the racetrack to my love for the women, vampirish as they were, who'd sprung from the pari-mutuel concourse whenever winning entered my billfold.

I told her all this, then asked if we couldn't go in on the iguana together, fifty-fifty. "Truth is," I said, "I came to the shop looking for a pet, but I had a case of the panics in there and, to be honest, I'm not sure I'm ready to care for any creature, no matter how lowly. But if we shared the caretaking . . . I mean, kept it at your place. So that if I fucked up, it would still be in good hands, what I'm saying is, that might be something I could do."

"How much time would you want to spend with it?" she asked.

"Just an hour or two a week." I assured her that I wouldn't come by without arranging my visit with her beforehand and that should she ever want me to stay away, I would respect her wishes.

"I have two questions," she replied.

"Fair enough," I said.

"How long have you been clean?"

I smiled at my accomplishment. "A hundred eighteen days," I said. "Not only that, I've driven a bakery truck for over half of them."

"So you've been employed for about two months?" she asked and I nodded. "My second question. You said you freed yourself from two great loves. What I want to know is which was harder, the racetrack or the women?"

"The racetrack," I replied. "The women was easy."

My answer seemed to satisfy her. "Well okay then," she said. "Let's go get our baby."

"I'm serious," I tell Geena. "A new set of nails would look sexy on you. Why not make an appointment for a fitting tomorrow?"

I carry our daughter to the bedroom, kiss her forehead, and set her down in a crib festooned with plastic animals—a frog, porpoise, and sea turtle that dangle above her in a mobile. In the mornings when sunlight filters through our curtains, Geena will poke the animals so they spin or bounce on their elastic lines. She says that when she does this Tina Louise's eyes open wide and in them she can see miniature reflections so precise they mesmerize her: the particular shade of green of the frog's skin, the exact angle of the porpoise's dorsal fin. Only more so, Geena tells me, a great deal more so. It's as if, Hank, it takes those eyes to get everything right. If she picks our daughter up, she can see in her eyes the hallway into our living room and half of the large glass terrarium in which we house our eastern corn snake, western milk snake, and three varieties of rat snake. It's as if, Hank, she says, I'm glimpsing a cleaner, clearer world than the one we live in.

I crawl under a single sheet in under-shorts I've worn since six p.m., when I first put Tina Louise to bed, having bathed and fed her, showered and eaten. A dead friend of mine once said that quitting heroin is like being at the beach during a heat wave, but you're allergic to water and can't tolerate even a few drops dribbled on your toes. All I know is when I close my eyes I don't believe sleep will ever overtake me; for this reason, I'm rarely upset at being awoken. But tonight Geena doesn't even pretend to want to let me sleep. There's the clunk of the empty ice milk tub hitting the trash bin, the bathroom light, shaven into a laser by jambs and sashes, beaming across my face, then Geena's knees thudding the tiles on either side of the toilet bowl. When her retching begins, I pray our neighbors will sleep through it, the gagging and high-pitched wheezes between heaves, the nightly spectacle Geena has made of her bulimia since the birth of our daughter.

What sounds like a shoe clops against the Weavers' side of the wall, a few inches above my head, and I rise from our bed and walk the hallway to the bathroom. Geena is hunched over the porcelain, her elbows cocked on the buffed white rim. When I ask her if I might fix her a cup of tea, she fires me a sidelong glance, fingers the back of her throat. It's then that one of the Weavers—either Ted or Marilyn—throws what sounds like an ashtray against the wall, and Geena hollers at them, "Can't you hear I'm sick, goddamn it?"

"You're sick every night!" Dick Henderson hollers back in his tired drawl. "And every night you subject the entire complex to it!"

"Then call the super!" Geena returns. Splotches of perspiration stain the ribbing of her halter-top. With each convulsion, her shoulder blades shimmy and the sides of her gut curl up under the lower hem. Kneeling beside her, I brush her hair away from her face, but a few brittle strands remain pasted to her skin.

"Don't look at me when I'm purging, Hank," she says. "It isn't comforting."

"Then why'd you leave the door open?" I ask.

"Because I wanted you to see that my condition isn't improving, that it's getting worse."

"I think you need to see someone," I say. "A doctor or therapist. Some problems are larger than us, honey."

"You'd like that, wouldn't you?" Geena replies. "My head shrunk and my body just getting bigger and bigger."

"Now, honey," I say, "there's nothing wrong with being a little overweight. More people are than aren't. It's nothing to be ashamed of."

"But I'm not most people," she says. "Inside, I'm thin."

"Tell me how I can help."

"By being in love with me, Hank," she answers. "By being head over heels in love with me."

"I am in love with you," I say.

"Then why don't I feel loved?" she asks.

"I don't know," I say. "I honestly don't know." And I don't.

From what I imagine to be a mirror image of our own flimsy pipes and plumbing, I hear Lana, Dick's wife, speaking to Geena: "Barf, baby. Chuck it up. So we can all go back to bed." We see these people leave and return, Lana in her Mazda, Dick in his Dodge, but outside our apartment we don't address them and avoid eye contact. I step into the hallway, shut the bathroom door behind me and, in the silence between gasps, hear our daughter murmuring in her sleep. If there be a God, I say to myself, He will not let her wake. Then the toilet flushes, and a *whoosh* of water through a too-small flange, this succeeded by the wail of a corroded ball cock, set off screams so shrill no narcoleptic could doze through them. Soon Tina Louise is back in my arms, jiggling up and down in her ecologically-friend-ly equivalent of Huggies. "Don't cry," I tell her. "Every-thing's fine. Daddy's here." I hold her next to her man-in-the-moon nightlight, my voice calm, assuring, yet her shrieks emerge with such force I cannot imagine a radio the same size producing a louder, more grating noise. From the west I hear Marilyn Weaver call her husband Ted an insensate, chauvinistic, baseball cap-wearing lout; from the east, Dick Henderson telling his wife Lana she's not to go anywhere without his permission—not to the market, not to the bowling alley, not to her goddamn sister's to borrow a Kotex. The volley of insults and accusations resumes on account of us, a nightly call and response between parties who cannot hear each other, though we can. We're right in the middle. "Shhh," I whisper to our baby, though with our neighbors in the throes of problematic marriages, the entire question of whether she quiets or not is moot.

In the midst of one of our baby's most blood-curdling wails, Geena steps from the darkness of the hallway into our bedroom, her face scrubbed ragged with a loofah, her cheeks puffy and orange in the glow from the nightlight. "Hand her over," she says.

"She'll stop," I say. "Just you wait."

"Give her here," Geena demands, and when I comply, she says, "Jesus, Hank, anyone would think you'd provided the sperm and egg both." She lifts a corner of her halter top, exposing a gangly breast, and I can't help wondering if it's healthy for our baby to be nourished by a mother who so regularly depletes her own body of nutrients.

"You've got to drop it, Geena, this binging and purging. It can't be good for our little one."

"Great. I've got a confirmed heroin addict telling me what's healthy." Tina Louise turns her pert lips toward Geena's nipple—mouth and nipple so close in color and texture it's difficult to say where one ends and the other begins. But our daughter, at least, is quiet.

"I've been clean 746 days," I say.

"You want a medal," she says, "or a chest to pin it on?"

"I'd take the chest," I say, "if it meant I could nurse our little one."

"My God, you are a piece of work. Now go make me that tea like you promised."

From my first visit to her apartment, Geena made no mystery of enjoying my company. Phoning ahead to set up an appointment, I had asked that she hold off feeding the iguana so that I might have some small thing to do while there, some small responsibility to meet that might tell me I was fit to assume a place, however humble, in humanity's evolution from cave-dwelling predators into a race capable of caring for one another. I told her her presence in the apartment was of no concern to me, though if she feared being robbed she could be there if she wished. She told me she would like to be there if only to witness my first steps toward becoming more fully human.

When I arrived, Geena set two salads on the kitchen table, one of romaine, spinach, and mushrooms, the other a few shredded creosote leaves in a restaurant ramekin. I recognized the leaves because I had eaten them myself on the long, catatonic walks I took while waiting for an atomic detonation to deliver me from my illness.

"You said on the phone that you wanted to feed her," Geena said. "So I went ahead and prepared what she likes to eat."

"She?" I said, for I could've sworn the iguana we'd purchased was male.

"Tina Louise," Geena replied. "I named her after the actress who played Ginger on Gilligan's Island."

"I remember Tina Louise," I said. "Always pampering herself, fixated on the Professor."

Geena smiled as she handed me the smaller salad. "Well, this Tina Louise prefers insects, but give her these for starters. If she doesn't eat them, we'll catch her some flies."

She walked me to the living room where a large glass terrarium sat on a plywood shelf supported by cinderblocks. Through the front of the enclosure I could see the layers of potting soil and pebbles with which she'd lined the base. On one side she'd planted a cactus. On the other she'd stacked three of four slabs of yellow granite. For several long moments I searched for the iguana without success; then, in the time it takes eyes to adjust after exposure to sunlight, her form coalesced on the flat rocks. "Lord, she's beautiful," I said, and she was—gold spots that turned the color of blood as they progressed the length of her and a gold stripe of pointed scales that descended from her hooded collar to the tip of her tail. At the pet shop, I admit, I hadn't really *seen* her.

"What do I do?" I asked.

"Just dump them in," Geena said, removing a lid she'd fashioned out of picture frame and screen. "She won't eat the leaves out of your hand, if that's what you're hoping. I think she needs to feel that she's found the food herself."

I tipped the ramekin upside down and watched the flakes flutter onto the rocks and pebbles, then waited for Tina Louise to make a move toward her food. I saw an eyelid shut and reopen, but the rest of her remained perfectly still, as if provender from heaven were about as extraordinary as air. "Don't feel bad," Geena said. "I haven't seen her eat yet either. I keep track of the leaves I drop in, so I know she isn't starving herself, but she's very private about mealtimes." She reached into the tank and scooped Tina Louise up in her palm. "Why don't you two get acquainted," she said, placing the iguana on my sleeve. "I'm going to finish making dinner."

When Geena left the room, I sat down in an easy chair with Tina Louise still clinging to my shirt. At an earlier time, I would've looked at such an exotic creature and asked myself how much she would've fetched on the black market. Now I could appreciate the trust another living thing had placed in me—her cool, dry tail against my forearm and the pain, not unbearable, of her claws digging into my arm through the thin weave. Heroin addicts never entirely buck their cravings, and as I sat there I wanted nothing more than to stick myself with a warm hypodermic. Yet, with Tina Louise apparently as comfortable hanging onto me as she had been upon the rocks in her terrarium, I wanted to meet her expectations for those rocks and, in so doing, appropriate for myself the power inherent in all inanimate things simply to be.

I did not so much as blink as I held her. The only sounds I heard were the creaks of my ribs as my lungs expanded and contracted and, from somewhere deep inside me, the perfectly modulated pulsations of my heart. After awhile, I gently plucked Tina Louise from my sleeve and carried her back across the room to her terrarium. Then I returned her to her granite slab and replaced the lid, thinking how fortunate it was that Geena and I had met and that she had agreed to our caretaking arrangement.

In the kitchenette, I told Geena that our visit had been a huge success and that I would like to come over again in three days. "No problem," she replied, and we settled on a time for my next visit.

"So I guess I'll be leaving," I said.

"Wait," she said. "You can't leave yet. All the food I made. Look." Beside the bowl of mixed greens rested a pitcher of iced tea, a pan of lasagna, and a basket of French bread wrapped in a paper towel. It was then that I understood that the blush she'd applied to her cheeks and the mascara with which she'd thickened her lashes, the shiny red blouse she wore just open enough to provide a glimpse of her red lace push-up bra hadn't been meant for a special someone, perhaps on his way across town.

"You made supper for us," I said, fearing in her offering more responsibility than I was ready to take on.

"The food won't poison you," Geena said.

"It isn't the food I'm worried about," I said. "It's our caretaking arrangement. I don't want to see it ruined by friendship."

"Ruined?" Geena asked. "By friendship?"

"You heard me," I said. "Friends narc on you.

Friends—"

"So a friend narced on you," she said, " and you're holding a grudge."

"No," I said. "I narced on a friend and he died in prison."

Geena sat down in a chair and eyed the table of food. "The dinner doesn't have to be the start of a friendship. It doesn't have to be the start of anything. We don't even have to talk."

"All right," I said. "I'll stay as long as we don't talk."

And for a time we didn't talk. For a time, the only sounds were the tings of our forks against our plates. The Geena confessed between forksful, "I wish I could keep quiet, but I can't. I have to tell you how impressed I was by your honesty at the espresso bar. It's all I've thought about, and I want you to know I think it's admirable what you're doing."

"There's nothing admirable about it," I said. "I'm just trying to take my mind off what I want more than unilateral disarmament or global peace."

"Then I won't ask you to talk about it," she said. "But there's something I want to share with you, so you'll know you aren't alone in your suffering."

"Each of us is alone in our suffering," I replied.

She nodded. "I know."

"So I wouldn't advise you to share anything with me. Because I have a way of bringing out the worst in people."

"I'm bulimic," she said. "So I know what you're going through, at least in so far as I know what it's like to be obsessed by something. I mean, I'm always looking for ways to take my mind off being thin. I'll never be thin, just look at me, but telling myself to stop thinking about it is the same as thinking about it, and the harder I try, the worse it gets. I've been to counselors and support groups where all we talk about is self-image, which doesn't help. Probably I'd have better luck at AA meetings."

"What is bulimia?" I asked.

"You don't know? It's an eating disorder. I can't believe you've never heard of it." Geena wiped a tear from her cheek. "So I eat, sometimes I eat a lot. Then I make myself throw up. It's disgusting, I know." She laughed, her face flushed and tear-streaked. "Just hearing myself describe it makes me ashamed."

I knew what bulimia was, but I wanted to hear her describe it. "You ought to be ashamed," I said. "What you've described is disgusting. You said so yourself."

I stood up to leave.

"I warned you," I said.

I set a pot of water on the stove. To each of our mugs I add a 1/2 teaspoon of acidophilus complex powder, a full teaspoon of folic acid with B12, 30 milligrams of zinc, and a ginseng teabag. According to Geena, these homeopathic remedies help the body to rebuild and normalize damaged nerve structures, promote cellular healing, and alleviate anxiety—which, Lord knows, I'm all for. Our tea made, I carry them into the living room where Geena sits nursing our baby under a reading lamp, stroking Tina Louise's curls with nails as glossy and red as Valentine's Day cutouts.

On the floor lies the wrapper from a ten-piece set of press-ons. "Those are some fancy nails," I say and make a show of admiring them, examining four at a time in the flat of my palm, when in truth they make me uneasy. Were Tina Louise to suddenly need me, she might be shredded by nails like those.

"I'll have you know, they're only a third the length of the ones I'm going to have put on at the manicurist's," Geena replies.

"I'm sure they'll look nice on you," I say, though I'm scared by the thought of talons even longer and sturdier than the ones she's wearing.

"Oh, quit being supportive," Geena says. "That's all you ever are. Supportive."

"Why don't you let me hold Tina Louise for awhile?" I ask.

"Why don't you busy yourself with one of your other Tina Louisas?" Geena replies.

I sit down on the Davenport, watched as I am by our gopher tortoise, indigo snake, ringneck snake, Mediterranean gecko, northern slimy salamander, Sonoran desert toad, green anole, earless lizard, barking treefrog, and greater siren. In our living room we house over twenty species of reptile and amphibian, each named Tina Louise and brought home to me by Geena, but cared for by me alone. Though each has proven more useful to me than my rehab clinics and twelve-step programs, all pale in comparison to the vast and humbling universe I behold in our infant daughter.

"You know," Geena says, "I gave you creatures to care for when what I wanted was for you to care for me."

"I care for you," I say.

"You pretend to," she says.

She may be right. But I ask you, isn't everything we do pretend until we get it right? Above us the fraternity brothers dribble a basketball on the floor of their apartment. In the bedroom, I put on a work shirt, trousers, a pair of boots.

"I had a dream last night," Geena says when I return to the living room. "I dreamt that Tina Louise was a grown woman, and that I was still breast-feeding her. It was a lovely dream—her eyelids closed, her adult head cradled in my arms, her lovely mouth moving from one nipple to the other. I could've stayed in the dream forever, feeling milk pass from my body to hers, both of us slender, beautiful."

"I'm leaving for work," I say.

"An hour early?" Geena says. "Don't tell me you have a sweetheart warming a bed for you somewhere."

I sit down beside her on the arm of the easy chair. "No, honey," I say, "there's no sweetheart warming a bed for me."

"It wouldn't surprise me if there were," she says.

"If I had a sweetheart," I say, "she'd be you, and we'd have a baby together, and we'd live in a house in the Heights, and we'd have neighbors who kept to themselves, and we'd have nice cars, and no financial worries, and eighteen years to decide whether to send our baby to Harvard or Yale."

With each bounce of the ball the ceiling pulsates like a heart, and as I wrap my arms around my wife,

I try to imagine that she is the actual Tina Louise, the actress who played Ginger on *Gilligan's Island*, with skin the same as hers, with hair, and eyes, and lips, and tits the same as Ginger's, but as I stare at Geena's nails it is an iguana that she becomes, a baby iguana that our infant daughter becomes, and I know that neither is safe as long as I am near, that I am as likely to squeeze the breath from their lungs as I am to protect them from harm.

Spoils

If the P. T. Cruiser wasn't returned by six, a late fee would be charged to my credit card, which I had maxed out treating my fiancée Y. and daughter Lara to a three-night Las Vegas getaway that had featured five-star dining, shows by Celine Dion and Blue Man Group, water slides, babysitters, and enough top-shelf liquor served in martini glasses to bankrupt a small nation. It was five-fifteen when I pulled into the Chevron near my apartment. Lara, four, sat in an infant carrier belted into the backseat examining illustrations in *Eloise Goes to Paris* like an interior decorator staring at wallpaper, with a skeptical fingertip pressed to her cheek.

"Honey," I said, "do you need to use the restroom?"

"No thank you," she replied, glancing at me in the rearview mirror. A gorgeous child with oat blond hair and irises the color of blue curaçao, she turned heads wherever she went. Though she had more of my looks than her mother's, no modeling scout had ever approached me, and her mother and I, when we talked, discussed the wisdom of subjecting any child, even one as headstrong as ours, to an industry that bred the very vanity on which it fed.

For sixty miles Y. and I had both needed to use the restroom, which was why we were filling the tank before unloading the car at the apartment, which we would have to do in record time to get the car back to the rental agency by closing time. Y., too, was stunning, a former student of mine who'd supported herself as a car show model and cocktail waitress in Dallas while studying for her Ph.D. in postmodern literature in Denton. Once wed, we could petition the very Department that had awarded her a Bachelor's degree Summa Cum Laude to hire her on a spousal line. I confess I liked that she wore black exclusively, rare in Tempe, that her wardrobe formed a draping void of satin, sequins, Dacron, and lace in the closet, that she dressed more formally than I did. Six of the thirteen chapters of her dissertation, each devoted to a different living obscure poet, had been published as articles in scholarly journals, and three New York publishers had expressed interest in the memoir she was writing about being raped at nineteen and again at twenty-three.

I swiped my emergency credit card, punched in my zip code, and fit the nozzle into the gas tank. As I was selecting the grade, my daughter called to me through the Cruiser's open rear window. "Actually, I do need to, I do."

"Okay, sweetheart."

Y. was between pump islands, her pellucid legs and arms stark as checkers on a racing flag. "Darling," I called to her, and as she spun on high heels between the grille of a rusting Chevy pickup and the bumper of a Winnebago, she was hard not to notice, swirling black hair, halter top, and bubble skirt all of a piece. "Lara has to go after all. Could you . . .?"

The words barely out, Y. was back at the car, freeing Lara from bondage meant to protect her. Doomed, it seemed, to choosing the gas nozzle that didn't catch, I fiddled with the trigger on the spout and squeezed my legs together. All the while I kept vigilant watch on the two women I loved most in the world as they crossed a concrete apron spotted with antifreeze and motor oil like any mother and daughter anywhere. As if by divine intervention, the regulator clip took, and I reached the Redi-Mart's plate glass door as a man about my age slipped inside in front of me. Tall, in cowboy boots and a western shirt decorated with lucky sevens and tumbling dice, he rounded the Icee dispenser in five strides and was at the men's room door. "Looks like I won," he said with a laugh, a gold incisor glinting between his unshaved cheeks. Beyond him lay a single toilet and sink.

When the door closed, I jogged in place in the wake of his stale cologne. The toilet flushed, but the door remained shut, and I pictured him before the mirror applying pomade to his salt and pepper pompadour, flossing egg salad from between his yellowing caps, scouring his grease-stained knuckles with strings of pink liquid soap. Had evil not flickered in his dark countenance? I'd filled Lara's plastic swimming pool with a garden hose in less time than it took him to freshen up. When at last the door opened, he winked at me as if letting me in on a private joke. "She's all yours," he said. Tears brimming, I rushed past him unzipping my fly. My eternal salvation, should it come to pass, would not be as sweet.

Once relieved, I stepped into the concession area as Lara raced up to me holding a container of Icebreakers, tropical flavored sours for which I, too, had acquired a

173

taste. "Mommy always buys me these," she exclaimed. When she was done eating the candies, Lara would put jacks and things in the round plastic containers they came in. Behind her the man who had beaten me to the men's room, all whiskered dimples and gleaming bourbon-colored teeth, was chatting up Y.

"No she doesn't. Now put them back where you found them," I said.

This sort of thing happened all the time. Whenever I turned away, men— "yoodles" Y. called them—materialized out of nowhere and laid on the charm. For the most part I tolerated them—none were ever going to be with a woman like Y.—and in moments of academic high mindedness I even considered their sexual overtures and overt propositions forms of flattery. But this was the first time it had happened in the presence of my daughter.

"What did that guy say to you in there?" I asked Y. when we were all three back in the car.

"Something about stepmothers getting a raw deal," she said.

"Asshole," I said.

"What did you say?" Lara piped from the back seat.

"Nothing, pumpkin." There was no length, it seemed, to which these guys wouldn't go to sow rancor among couples who were apparently happy.

"How did he know you weren't Lara's mother?"

Y. gawked at me as if I were as dense as a college freshman. "Spense, my question for you is why in the world would he?"

At the apartment, having returned Lara to her mother and the car on time, Y. and I put away our spoils—Flamingo Hotel shot glasses and Paris Hotel schooners, a black party dress Y. had found discounted from $599 to $299 at a boutique in The Venetian and a Hawaiian shirt (for which I'd paid full price) from the gift shop in Mirage, matches from Planet Hollywood, and a coffee table book chronicling in photographs Las Vegas's history from the Twenties to the present. As I fired up the grill for steaks thawing in the microwave, Y. made us a pitcher of mojitos with mint leaves picked from our small herb garden. She brought out the drinks on a glass tray as I dropped a pair of aged filets onto the fire. Everyone but us seemed to resent that we were in love, and at times I wondered if home were the only place we could enjoy it. The guy at the Chevron had been preceded by many just like him, and I didn't relish the thought that he would be anteceded by many more.

"Do you think there's anything you do, honey," I asked judiciously, "consciously or unconsciously, that encourages the yoodles?"

As our meat sizzled, Y. and I sat side by side on a wicker love seat with our feet on a table of slate, I in cutoffs and an old Waylon Jennings t-shirt, she in a black lace slip-dress.

"Besides breathe?" she replied.

I took a sip of my mojito. "I never dated anyone who drew such attention."

"You were married for ten years to a plain woman

the same age as you. Now you're marrying an attractive woman fifteen years your junior. A lot of men would kill to have what you have. Seeing us together triggers their blood lust. Don't you see that?"

"Older man, younger woman—it's practically a cliché," I said. "Are you saying every couple configured like us is as prone to harassment as we are?"

Y. shrugged and tossed back her black hair, which irritated me. When she was nineteen, her twenty-seven-year-old ex-boyfriend had shown up at her apartment the night after she'd broken up with him and raped her on her couch at gunpoint. Four years later she was raped again, this time by a stalker on a parking ramp in downtown Dallas. Now, six years after that, she was writing about both incidents with a stylish dispassion and limpidity that enabled her to find comedy in the horror. I liked what I'd read of it, disturbing as its subject matter was.

"You've never been involved with a rape victim, have you, Spense?" she said.

"Not that I know of," I conceded.

"My first rapist told me he was performing a public service. My second that he was powerless against my charms."

"Meaning?"

"My first rapist changed something in me. It's as if he planted a device and now I emit a signal of a particular wavelength."

"Surely the device can be removed," I said, respecting her analogy.

"How?"

176

I shrugged. I didn't know. Y. had no interest in psychotherapy, believing it anathema to her creative and scholarly pursuits and a racket to boot. "I'm just sick and tired of men of every stripe coming up to us, is all."

"Every man I've ever dated said the exact same thing, Spense."

"So there's nothing we can do about it? Is that what you're saying?"

"I guess I could uglify myself," she replied. "I could put on two hundred pounds and wear a romper, and far fewer would be drawn from the woodwork, but is that what you want, Spense? For me to be completely broken?"

"Of course not."

"See? You're as drawn to the signal as they are. You don't want it muted either."

I thought of all the toys, many of them missing parts, Lara had outgrown. The apartment was filled with turtles that no longer giggled, frogs that no longer recited the alphabet, Hello Kitty! everything. Loathe to part with any of one of them, I feared the more sophisticated toy that would replace it.

If Y. were right, and I believed she was, then I loved something in her that would kill me in a daughter.

I'm OK, You're OK

When I opened the passenger door of his Plymouth station wagon, the clown in the driver's seat turned to me. "Tell me you aren't going to murder me," he said.

"OK," I said.

"Now that we have that settled," he said, "you might as well stow your pack in the back."

With an oversized prosthetic thumb he signaled over his polka-dotted shoulder. His other hand rested firmly on the steering wheel. Back then I was afraid of no one. I was twenty, had dropped out of college, and was hitchhiking to Alaska to make my fortune seining salmon, though I knew next to nothing about it. Earlier in the day, my mother had dropped me off on an I-94 entrance ramp thirty miles north of the Twin Cities and sped away in her Volvo sedan, hurling gravel behind her. Neither she nor my father had wanted me to go and had tried to dissuade me from leaving by imagining all sorts of gruesome scenarios. What if someone put a gun to my head? What if I was in a car with jerry-rigged locks? What if I was picked up by an Ed Gein who could only see me as bowls and lampshades and furniture upholstery? Always the what-ifs returned to Ed Gein. My father, an M.D., had grown up forty miles north of Ed's hometown of Plainfield, Wisconsin, and from this believed he'd acquired unique insight into the workings of Ed's brain. *I went to school with guys just like Ed. A guy like Ed will stop at nothing. You know*

178

this, right?

"Feel free to rearrange my stuff," said the clown. "I know it's a mess back there."

The backseat was folded down, the cargo area heaped with the props of his trade. Balloon pumps, squirting cameras, and hula-hoops. Devil sticks, dove pans, and linking silks. Blooming bouquets, wilting carnations, and spinning plates. Beneath all the novelties and gags, which I swept gently to the side, lay flat cardboard boxes containing electrical fuses of various types and ratings.

As I climbed in next to him on the passenger seat, the clown said, "Gig in Fargo. Kid's seventh birthday party."

I pulled the passenger door shut. "Cool," I said.

"You like clowns?" he asked as we gathered speed on the shoulder, then merged with the northwestern-bound traffic. "You find them entertaining, do you?"

"Not especially," I replied, which brought a chuckle from him.

"You're not alone, buddy," he said, "and that's coming from someone who subsidizes his income handily by performing as one. Why, you wouldn't believe how many parents tell me, usually as they're cutting my check, mind you, how creepy my performance was. But they don't know creepy. I know creepy."

"What's creepy?" I asked.

"You wanna know what's creepy? What's really creepy?" With the same rubber thumb, which had been molded to appear infected, with a dark red abscess to the right of the nail, he pointed at his forehead, painted white to an orange wig that gave one the impression of a scalp on fire. "What's going on in here, behind the makeup, behind the flesh and bone." He turned to me and improvised the snarl of a cornered cat, though his pair of dimples and heart-shaped smile remained as fixed as his round, red nose. "Scaring you yet?"

"You don't scare me," I said.

"Not even an iddy-biddy bit?" he replied.

"Sorry," I said.

"Be a tough guy then," he said. "See if I care."

Earlier in the day I'd been picked up by a divorce attorney on a Kawasaki KZ650 and a soybean farmer in a '57 pickup. The former had taken me sixty miles, the latter a mere twenty-three, though the amount of time I'd spent with each seemed about the same. The divorce attorney had treated me to a hamburger, fries, and Coke at a Dairy Queen buffeted on three sides by a granite quarry, and as he told me about his wife and how he could no longer trust her because of an affair she'd had thirteen years before while he was serving in Nam, an affair he'd only just learned about recently, in the distance boulders rolled from the tip of a conveyor belt through the elevated gate of a finishing mill, emitting tiny puffs of smoke. "I'd like to kill her," he said.

The soybean farmer had referred to his truck as his "buggy," which put me in mind of the black horse-drawn carriages seen cantering on the shoulders of highways outside Amish settlements, which was, I imagined, how we appeared to the motorists careering past us like guided missiles. He drove for a time in the right lane, then on the shoulder, pebbles ricocheting off the underbody like marbles in a pachinko machine, as if *our* interstate didn't quite match up with everybody else's. Even with the windows open, the cab reeked of cigarettes, though the ashtray contained no butts or ash; indeed, it sparkled, as if recently removed, scrubbed, sanitized, and burnished, below a chrome and glass dashboard thick with dust. When I asked him about it, he told me that at seventy-seven he'd finally kicked a Viceroy habit that had put his wife in the ground earlier that year at seventy-two. Now I was riding with a clown who found his own thoughts scary.

"The truth is," the clown said, "nobody likes a clown. We stay in business because we're like fruitcake. Nobody likes fruitcake either. But I'll tell you what. When was the last time you heard of a fruitcake company filing bankruptcy?"

"Never," I said.

"My point exactly," he said. "When the power goes out, as the Bible says it most certainly will, and the world no longer has use for electricians such as myself, those that survive the nuclear holocaust will sit around campfires eating fruitcake and laughing at clowns, you may rest assured."

"You're an electrician by trade?"

"Fully bonded, licensed, and insured." He nodded at the sign I'd fashioned out of cardboard, my destination, 'ALASKA,' cradled in my lap. "So tell me, why in God's name would someone like yourself be on his way to some place like that? Winters here not cold enough for you?" He laughed at his own tired joke. From Halloween to Easter, Minnesotans asked each other if the weather was cold enough, as if the subzero wind chills and pelting snowfalls were a quaint, refreshing summertime quaff. I'd had enough of it and was going to a place where quaintness wasn't a virtue and the wilderness was as yet unspoiled.

"I don't mind the cold," I replied.

"OK, tough guy, be that way. I'm putting in overtime over here trying to make conversation and you aren't giving me much to work with. Out of politeness— politeness, I say—I asked you a simple question. Why, I asked, in God's name would someone like yourself be on his way to some place like that? Because, I gotta say, the type of person you're likely to meet up there— granted, this is largely speculation on my part—is someone who couldn't make things happen down here in the Lower Forty-Eight where most Americans live, or someone who's running from something—get my drift?—the law, a stigmatizing criminal past, debt, a ball-busting spouse, child support—or, more likely, some combination of the above. I'll cut to the chase, which of the aforementioned fuckups are you?"

I had to laugh, and when I did, the clown said, "A humble clown has brought you mirth. All is right with the world."

And the world did seem right. The earth passed beneath us. A median of thick mowed grass undulated before us to the horizon. Stands of forest advanced and receded. A farmhouse and barn swung by as if on a Lazy Susan, as did a corrugated warehouse, a radio tower, a corn harvester stalled in a field, one vision succeeding another, each as vaporous as a cloud formation. I was a garden-variety fuckup at best. I hadn't killed anyone, knocked some chick up, or done prison time. I hadn't yet made a total mess of things. My girlfriend had broken up with me, this was true, and in my grief over losing her I'd fallen asleep on railroad tracks at two in the morning, believing that when I awoke I'd be free of earthly torment, but to my credit I'd eaten hallucinogenic mushrooms with friends at a vernal equinox party that night, and neither I nor my therapist believed I was at risk of a second attempt.

At Saint Olaf College, where I'd completed four semesters of its premed program with barely passing grades, I'd been anxious, unsure of myself, miserable, but from the moment I picked myself up from the crossties, my life having been spared by dumb luck, it was as if a veneer had been stripped from it and I could make as much or as little of it as I liked. My life was my own, and if it ended abruptly, who cared if an Ed Gein stitched my skin to the back of a chair or hung my skull on a bedpost? Who cared if my organs chilled on a shelf of his refrigerator or my navel weighted the drawstring of his window shade?

I said to the clown, "I'm a fuckup all right, but that isn't why I'm on my way to Alaska. I'm on my way to Alaska because I've always wanted to go there, ever since I was a little kid."

"So I'm helping you to realize a dream? A fantasy? That it?"

"And I thank you for it," I replied.

"Goody gumdrops," the clown exclaimed. "Shoot your wad all over the final frontier, laddy. White it out.

Cover the mountaintops. Bugger the elk and moose. Would you like a breath mint?"

I told him no thanks. "Take a breath mint," he said and shook a roll of Certs at me, the wrapping peeled back to the next speckled lozenge. I took it, popped it in my mouth as if to challenge my parents' edict against accepting food from strangers and felt relieved at the first taste of wintergreen. Even so, as I chewed and swallowed, I expected heavy-lidded drowsiness and loss of consciousness to follow, for by then I wasn't sure the clown wasn't an Ed Gein or that my father had been wrong to believe the world full of them, all quietly blending in, their telltale quirks conveniently overlooked by those unfortunate enough to know them. And sure enough, as if by the power of suggestion, I felt myself growing tired. Really tired, as if I hadn't slept in days.

"So what are you?" he asked. "One of those trust-fund babies? One of those snotty rich kids who never has to work?"

"Why do you ask?"

"The whole time we've been talking I haven't once heard you say what you plan to do up there . . . FOR A LIVING! So I says to meself, perhaps the bloke is independently wealthy and doesn't need to wear the yoke of labor. But then, says meself to I, it isn't as if he's driving a Maserati. He isn't even driving a Plymouth. He's isn't driving anything. He's hitchhiking."

I answered what I thought the safer of his two questions. "I plan to find work on a salmon seiner. Deck-handing. I hear there's good money in it, if you get on the right boat, with the right skipper."

Residents of the suburb of south Minneapolis where I'd grown up, Edina, were known throughout the state as 'cake-eaters.' A high percentage of my friends' fathers occupied executive positions with 3-M, I.B.M., and Control Data or were attorneys or physicians. I didn't relish the lambasting I'd receive if the clown learned this.

But I wasn't a trust-fund baby. Since school had let out, from sunup till sundown my best friend Todd and I had painted houses in our neighborhood—it was why the backs of my arms and legs were pecan and the fronts were as pale as peanut shells—and the three thousand dollars in twenties I carried in my wallet I'd earned, as my father himself had said, the hard way. Still, even if my father had set up an account in my name, which he hadn't, he would've closed it long before I left for Alaska. To him my undertaking, if one could call it such, was the apotheosis of dimwittedness.

A cockeyed grin formed in the Valentine's Day heart that encompassed the clown's cheeks and chin. "Leave it to an electrician to discover the flaw in your plan, the wrench in your works, the fly in your soup."

"What's the flaw?" I asked, though I didn't doubt my plan had one.

"Today is the first of August, am I correct? Even if you hitchhiked three hundred miles per day, you might make it to Alaska, depending on where in Alaska you're going, in time to fish for maybe, if you're lucky, twenty-four hours. Salmon are a migratory fish, dinglefritz. From June to August, when the salmon are swimming back to the rivers from whence they came, they're fished in three to five day openings set by the Department of Fish and Game. One doesn't go to Alaska in August hoping to land a job on a salmon seiner. One goes in May." He tapped his forehead with his prosthesis, then inspected it to make sure that none of his face paint had rubbed off on it. A little had, which he wiped on his polka-dotted jumpsuit, a costume that so perfectly ensconced him it was impossible to tell if he was fat or thin, thirty-five or sixty. "And here I thought I was stupid."

In all of my arguments with my parents the question of timing had never come up. It made me feel sorry for us, as if the prize we'd sought had been devalued from the start by an inexplicable gap in our knowledge. I'd deployed every armament in my arsenal, as had they, yet to none of us had it occurred that the salmon season might be over by the time I got there. I didn't know what to say to the clown, only that I wouldn't be deterred from my final destination by such a small detail as a salmon's life cycle, that if I had to find other employment in Alaska until the salmon ran again, I would. And as I made my argument anew, this time to a person who might well have drugged me and whom I could not have picked out from a police lineup were I to survive the ride, I imagined my father returning from work with his collar unbuttoned and tie loosened, my mother overseeing pork chops sizzling in the electric fryer, scalloped potatoes browning in the oven, and fresh cucumbers and bell peppers my sister and brother were chopping for a garden salad.

Was my family talking about my absence, speculating about how far I'd traveled during my first day on the road, or had my father declared the subject verboten? I suspected the latter.

"You might," said the clown, "find work on a crab boat. Kings are fished in September and October, dungeness all winter long. It's why so many crab fishermen die. Boats are shellacked in ice and sink. A fisherman's boot gets caught in the ropes and a crab pot pulls him to the bottom of the sea. Four or five seconds is about as long as anyone can last in such water." He glanced at me with an appraising eye. "You don't look like you have what it takes to crab. If you'll pardon my saying so, you don't look like you have what it takes to fish either. You've been pampered. I can tell by your thin fingers and wrists. Where you from anyway? The Twin Cities? One of its suburbs? North Oaks maybe? Edina?"

My head was balanced precariously on my neck, fatigue having crept from my extremities inward and then upward. "So what makes you such an authority on Alaskan fishing?" I asked. I shook my head to keep from slipping into unconsciousness, focused on the hum of the air-conditioner, the rows of cornstalks spinning on either side of us like enormous helicopter blades, the long, late afternoon shadows cast by the power lines.

"I'm no authority," he replied, "except compared to you, which is funny, isn't it, considering you're the one going up there to deckhand and all."

"I guess it is," I said.

"I hope you don't think I'm trying to make you feel bad."

"I don't feel bad," I said.

"Not being cut out for the work we want isn't the worst thing."

"I wouldn't know," I said.

"No," he agreed, "you wouldn't."

"I'm just going to close my eyes for a moment," I said, "if you don't mind."

"Close your eyes, tough guy."

And as I fell asleep I thought of the railroad tracks on which I'd lain and how, miraculously, no harm had come to me.

When I awoke, we were leaving Moorhead and crossing the Red River of the North into North Dakota. "I've given some thought to your predicament," said the clown.

"Oh yeah?" I said, surprised I wasn't manacled to an operating table in a basement laboratory, surprised I'd awoken at all.

"I'll make you a proposition. You can be my apprentice. For the next nine months, I'll teach you everything an electrician needs to know and, as a special bonus, everything a clown needs to know as well. By next May, if you wish to continue on your way, at least you'll have two trades with which to support yourself."

Though I could not in my wildest dreams imagine accepting his offer, I said, "That's very kind of you."

"So what do you say?" he asked. "Do we have a deal? You'll be my helper, and in exchange you'll learn about capacitors and resistors and how to captivate a child with simple sleights-of-hand. You'll learn about plugs and wiring and the jokes that never fail to bring a child, even a sick one, joy."

"Thank you but no," I said.

My father had tried to persuade me to stay in Edina with the offer of a place to live while I reconsidered my options and decided whether Alaska was really for me. As far as I was concerned, he and the clown were making virtually the same appeal in virtually the same tone of voice.

"I'm worried about you, tough guy," said the clown. "I'd hate for anything bad to happen to you. You stick with me and you'll be better prepared for life's tough realities."

"If anything bad happens to me," I said, "you'll likely never know about it."

"True," he said, "but I have terrible misapprehensions. I *know* what's out there. You seem like a nice young man, but you're inexperienced, and you have no idea what danger you're in."

On the expressway it was rush hour, Fargoans entering and exiting the stream of traffic pretty much as they had at the end of every workday for decades and would, I imagined, for time ad infinitum, and while some glanced quickly at the clown driving the Plymouth before returning their gazes to the road, most took no notice of him.

"Listen," he said, "I've got to be at a kid's birthday party in twenty minutes. Why don't you perform as my assistant and we'll talk about this further after the gig?

I have a backup costume you can wear. The customer will get two clowns for the price of one. And we'll split my fee, seventy-thirty."

"I don't think so," I replied.

"How about sixty-forty?"

"Unh-unh," I said.

"All right then, we split it fifty-fifty. Agreed?"

I wagged my head. "You can let me out anywhere. You've driven me quite a stretch and for that I thank you."

"For *that* you thank me? For that *you* thank me? For that you *thank* me?"

He signaled his turn and pulled off the expressway into a business district. At a McDonalds he backed into a parking spot beside a dumpster. Two boys and a girl were climbing on a jungle gym in the play area, clearly visible through the Plymouth's windshield. "I need you to do one thing for me," he said. "One thing, to show your appreciation for all I've done, and tried to do, for you. Do you think you can do one thing?"

From the fly of his polka-dotted jumpsuit extended his fully erect penis, the only actual flesh disclosed by his entire costume.

"Will you please just kiss it," he asked. "You don't have to do anything else. Just kiss it. That's all I ask." I unlocked the passenger door and opened it. Before I could get out, he said, "Think of them." He nodded at the children at play. "If you can't find it in your heart to do this one thing for me, will you do it for them? To protect them? To keep them from harm?"

A couple years ago my daughter celebrated her fifth birthday. Her mother and I no longer lived together, but our breakup had been amicable enough for us to throw Lili a party together at one of Albuquerque's municipal parks, the one we decided upon roughly equidistant from our homes. All of Lili's prior birthdays had been small, private affairs, but her fifth struck us as a milestone, and we wanted to do something more lavish for her than we'd done in the past. Neither of us had much money to spend on it, and so in addition to the Ariel-themed birthday cake our daughter had requested, the requisite snacks and beverages, and the rental Ariel-themed jumping castle with which we hoped to surprise her, Amy and I surveyed our friends for talent and by the afternoon of the party had enlisted face-painters, a guitarist, a balloon artist, and, yes, a clown.

Easily twenty of Lili's preschool friends turned out for the event, all but two of them girls. My parents, having moved from Edina fifteen years before to a gated community south of Flagstaff, made the five-hour trip in their Acura. Amy's new boyfriend, a pony-tailed high school English teacher in his fifties, painted the faces of the little ones while Michelle, who was not yet my wife but would be in less than two years, phoned from Detroit for periodic updates. The celebration was, in short, a great success. Though storm clouds blew in during the middle of it and sprinkled on us, in New Mexico any rain was considered a blessing, and even when the jumping castle deflated due to a faulty gen-

191

erator, all the children were laughing as they escaped from beneath its collapsing nylon ceiling through its maw-like portal.

Several of the students from the creative writing program in which I taught took me up on my invitation and arrived bearing five garbage bags filled with balloons sculpted into clearly recognizable animal shapes. One of their peers had done the twisting, something he'd once done professionally while working as a clown in a traveling Ukrainian circus. He wasn't, however, the one who had offered to perform a clown routine. The woman who had volunteered to do that was one of Amy's colleagues at the Bureau of Indian Affairs, a one-time opera singer from Saint Paul who, back when I'd been obliged to accompany Amy to Bureau functions, had taken wicked delight in poking fun at my "privileged upbringing" once she'd learned in which Minneapolis suburb I'd grown up. The truth was, I couldn't stand Phyllis, and took her cancellation due to laryngitis as another sign that God was smiling down on us. March 20th, the day of my daughter's birth, was also, coincidentally, the anniversary of my botched suicide attempt, and as one of Lili's friends' dads performed Dan Zanes' songs on a homemade guitar and children and adults gorged themselves on white cake and lemonade, I took stock, as I had on each of Lili's previous birthdays, of all that would not have been had I succeeded in taking my life.

That night I prepared my parents a supper of pan-seared flank steak and beer-battered onion rings and, because it was her birthday, macaroni and cheese for

Lili. Apropos of nothing, my father said, "That day you left us to hitchhike to Alaska, surely you couldn't have imagined that one day all of this would be yours."

What he meant by "this," I understood, was the life I'd somehow cobbled together out of nothing more than a desire to write.

"You're right," I said. "I couldn't."

For as I'd retrieved my backpack from the back of the clown's station wagon in Fargo, North Dakota nearly thirty years ago, the air was fragrant with the smell of cut hay, and as I walked back toward the interstate I couldn't imagine ever confiding in another person, much less putting it in writing, what had just happened, what I had and had not done.

At Night We Play Hearts

I had a good buzz going by the time I was dropped off in Gardiner, Montana by Wayne, a ranch hand who'd fished cans of Pearl from a Coleman cooler strapped into the bed of his pickup. Before that I'd smoked a bowl with two French-Canadian seminarians who'd played "Dinah-Moe-Humm" over and over on a boom-box inside their VW van, such that when they dropped me off at the turnoff for Pray and the head of a trail they were going to hike into the Absaroka Range, Frank Zappa's funk-inspired classic satire about a sexual dare gone wrong (or right, depending on how you looked at it) was grinding in my head and would be for days.

Inside Red's Blue Goose Saloon I ordered another Pearl. It was too early to hitchhike to the Boiling River Hot Spring, and I didn't relish the prospect of baking on Yellowstone's North Entrance Road. From where I sat Roosevelt Arch, two stone pillars supporting voussoir and spandrel, wavered in the distance like a mirage into which a person might vanish or from which rematerialize. Better to arrive at the hot spring at twilight, I told myself, as I had the previous summer when I'd stumbled onto an orgy and found myself naked in a natural bath with more than a dozen naked strangers, three-quarters of them female and all of them drunk or stoned or tripping.

That summer I'd worked for the Hamilton Stores Corporation selling fishing tackle, light groceries, and camping supplies to tourists staying at the Lake Campground and wouldn't have known about the spring at all—it wasn't officially designated on any map—if a hippie couple a few years older than me hadn't come into the store needing duct tape to mend a rip in the floor of their tent. The woman was slender and gorgeous with straight dark hair that fell to breasts covered by blue threadbare crepe and pupils contracted to the size of periods. The man looked both young and wizened, his eyes sparkling as if through his sun-bleached curls they saw what ordinary mortals could not. As I waited on them, he told me they had wintered in Big Bend National Park where at night they'd waded across the Rio Grande to the Mexican village of Boquias, purchased peyote buttons for six pesos a piece, and brought them back to the campground where they sold them at a small profit to other desert-worshipping longhairs who were either too timid or lazy to procure the contraband themselves.

"It was a trip, man," he kept saying, "a real trip," and each time the woman smiled at him with such deference, such total devotion, I couldn't help thinking of my girlfriend Johanna back in her dorm room at the University of Minnesota, setting up her electric hotplate, kettle, and assortment of teas in preparation for the fall semester. What this couple had was what I wanted for us, and if she could've only seen them for herself, I thought, she would've wanted it, too. But whenever we talked long distance on the phone, she seemed more interested in anabolism and catabolism than she did in us, more interested in the mysteries of the carbon cycle than in those of the self in relation to others.

"Got any more you want to sell?" I asked.

"More what?"

"Buttons," I whispered, aware of my boss, Big John, manning the counter where I'd left a rental fishing reel I was cleaning in parts on the glass. "You know, peyote."

"Oh man," said the dude, "we ate the last ones ourselves two nights ago. You should've been there."

"It was mind-altering," the woman agreed. "Mind-fucking-altering. The whole experience. Everybody naked and loving one another." She turned to her man, beaming.

"We have to go back there."

"We will, darling, we will," he replied, and that's when they told me about the hot spring, even drew an X on the map taped to the display case to identify precisely where I would find it.

And find it I did, on my next day off.

If 'orgy' was, in retrospect, overstating it, two couples were fucking in plain view of the rest of us, the men lying on their backs with their heads on rocks as the women they were with undulated on top of them, radiating waves that crested against our necks and chins. Nobody paid them any mind, so I didn't either, though it occurred to me that a woman could get pregnant from just sitting in such water. To my right and left, young people chatted about what an asshole somebody's foreman was, how rude a majority of tourists were, how hard it was to make any real money when vacationers to the park were such lousy tippers, and I gathered that nobody in the spring was remotely like the hippie couple that had directed me there; they were all like me, college kids on summer break, earning minimum wage cleaning guest cottages, waiting tables, ringing up postcards, snacks, and souvenirs. None of them had eked out livings transporting peyote buttons by moonlight across the Rio Grande, none of them.

As I stretched out my arms on boulders, a girl with wavy brown hair and a tan that started at her fingertips and ended just above her elbows backed into my shoulder and chest and treated them as her personal backrest. I wasn't complaining, and for a time we stayed like that. Then she spun in the water to face me and her nipples brushed against my thigh. "Hello there," she said. "Who are you?"

"Who are you?" I asked.

"I asked you first," she said, so I told her my name and Pauline told me hers, shaking my hand under the water. From Great Neck, New York, she was studying forestry at the University of Maine-Orono, she said, and working with the National Park Service as a Youth Conservation Corp volunteer, clearing trails and manning fire lookouts. Though the work wasn't as exciting as she'd hoped, it was all part of her plan to become a park ranger in Yellowstone. "I mean," she said and stood up on our rock ledge in nothing but a choker of cowry shells, "look around us. Who would want to be anywhere else?"

It was sunset, and as Pauline, to her knees in the pool, lifted her arms as if supplicating herself before

a benevolent God, reds, pinks, and violets highlight-
ed her hair. Rivulets, too, caught the last light as they
coursed along the small of her back and the backs of
her thighs. Even the couples fucking paused to register
their approval.

"Not me!" cried one of the men.

"Preach to us, Pauline!" cried one of the women.
"Give us your sermon on the mount!"

"All of us gathered here today," Pauline proclaimed,
"are the most blessed people on Earth."

"Amen, sister. Amen."

"God has seen fit," she said, "to bless us with one
another in a landscape fully imbued with His holiness,
mystery, and grace." Someone handed her a pint of Canadian Club, and as she tipped it to her lips, whiskey
dribbled down her chin. Beyond the Gardiner River, a
herd of bison lowed and stirred, an oil stain spreading
on black velour.

"It's a sin not to appreciate His majesty and splen-
dor."

"It's a sin not to appreciate yours," someone replied.

"Freddy," she said, "that you see God's handiwork in
so lowly a creature as I is pitiful if gratifying."

As people clapped and whistled, Pauline slipped
back into the pool, took another slug, and passed the
bottle to me. "Put your arm around me," she said. When
I did, she said, "Now hold me like you mean it." When I
complied with this request as well, she kissed my neck,
my ear, my hair as if starved for human touch. Our
mouths met, and I had to push her gently away. "Don't
tell me you have a girlfriend back home," she said.

What could I say? I did. But I didn't anymore. Johanna had broken up with me over the winter, citing "our irreconcilable visions of the future," and to show her I didn't need her or her ability to view all of life as particles, I'd dropped out of college and lit out for the west, Alaska my ultimate destination. But as I ordered up Pearl after Pearl at Red's Blue Goose Saloon, I imagined meeting up with Pauline at the hot spring a full year after meeting her there the first time. I'd slip into the water and take up residency beside her, and by my actions she would know that nothing stood between us now. I wouldn't have to hold her *like* I meant it, I *would* mean it, and if she meant for me to make love to her there in the spring in front of a dozen of her friends, I would.

My inhibitions sent adrift on a river of lager, I paid my bar tab, bought a pint of Canadian Club at the off-sale window and stuffed the bottle into a side pocket of my backpack. In a restroom I brushed my teeth and gargled with Listerine. For two and half days I'd been gassed with fossil fuel exhaust, and when I emerged from the spring, I would be newly baptized, Johanna and her love of organic molecular compounds no more a part of me than the grease lifted from my skin in a rainbow-colored slick and carried away by the river.

No sooner had I stuck out my thumb than I was picked up on the North Entrance Road by retirees Jake and Mildred. They were driving a camper with Kansas plates, Jake in the driver's seat in a tan windbreaker and navy blue 45th Airborne Division cap, Mildred in a red button-down sweater and pink nylon scarf. Though it was still in the mid-90s as the sun brushed the summit of Sepulcher Mountain five miles to the west, the cab was refrigerated to a temperature that would keep meat from spoiling.

"Welcome aboard," Jake said as I fell into the seat vacated by Mildred and wedged my backpack between my knees and the dash.

"You can put your pack in the back with me," Mildred said, crouched like a gnome between her husband and me, "if you think you'd be more comfortable."

"No thanks," I said and told them I'd be getting out a mile or two past the north entrance gate.

"Just give me the word," Jake said, "and I'll pull over."

"He loves to pull over. It's why it takes us so long to get here from Wichita every year."

"Mildred's right," Jake replied. "I like to feel the earth under my feet."

"Also Jake's bladder isn't what it once was," Mildred said.

"So you come to Yellowstone every summer?" I asked.

"Every summer," Jake replied.

"This will be our eighteenth," Mildred said.

"We love it," Jake said.

"We've made a lot of friends over the years," Mildred said.

"Got that right," Jake said.

"Nowadays we play a lot of cards. We don't explore the natural wonders like we used to."

"Speak for yourself, Mildred."

"Jake explores. I mainly visit with friends and catch up on gossip."

"And at night we play hearts," Jake said.

Once through the entrance gate, I kept an eye out for the unmarked parking lot and trail through the brush to the flat basalt boulders that concealed the spring from passing motorists. "That's my stop up ahead," I said. A camper like Jake and Mildred's was parked on the gravel.

"I'll be," Jake said as he pulled up alongside the other vehicle. "That's Bill and Sandy's. Mildred, take a look."

"Yep," Mildred confirmed. "I'd recognize it any-where."

Jake blared the car horn, but no one emerged from the shell. "Knowing them, they're probably out clod-hopping." He turned to me. "You sure this is where you want to be let out? There doesn't appear to be much out here."

If I told them about the spring, they might ask to come along. "I'm going to pitch a tent beside the Gardiner River," I said, "and meditate like Siddhartha."

"Well, if you run into Bill and Sandy," Mildred said, "don't let them talk your ear off."

"They're talkers, those two," Jake said.

As I followed the trail through bull grass to the spring, Frank Zappa's "Dyna-Moe-Humm" played in my head, confirming my belief that I was on my way to a bacchanal despite the camper abandoned where cars, jeeps, and motorcycles had once been parked hubcap-to-hubcap. The same herd of bison floated between river and butte, and the musky smells of pine and dung served to vaporize the year that had elapsed between my visits, such that when the trail descended between boulders and paralleled the flats and I glimpsed the outcropping of stones surrounding the pool, I wondered where all the lovely hedonists had fled, the couples fucking, Pauline and her drunken cohorts Colleen and Rachel who, when told I had a girlfriend back home, delighted in jiggling their breasts and taunting me with all that I was missing by remaining faithful.

Bathing in their place were Bill and Sandy, though neither said a word as I set my backpack in the dirt, dropped my drawers, and slid naked into the spring with them.

"Goddamn, it feels good to scrub off the sheep shit," I said. "Name's Wayne."

Probably they were as unhappy to see me as I was to see them, for in time Bill harrumphed and climbed from the water in his yellow swimming trunks, then helped Sandy out in her frilly turquoise one-piece. They had as much right to the palliative waters as anybody, and for that I resented them.

Time

Thirty years later, I've had a child with one woman and married another, and in truth I barely recognize the 'me' I was back then. What I remember about waking up beside the hot spring in the slanting light of dawn—the butte, the river, the rock on which I lay, my face mashed into a pillow fashioned out of an Icelandic wool sweater Johanna had given me for Christmas—was that everything seemed connected, interdependent. Maybe it was the times, but I believed that if a single blade of bull grass were erased—not plucked, shredded, smoked, or otherwise reconstituted, but separated from its existence atoms and all—earth and sky would fold into each other and become like cake batter, swirling and glutinous, no part recognizable from another.

My breath crystallized above me and dispersed. Across the river steam rose from the nostrils of bison and dispersed above the herd. From my backpack I withdrew my collapsible, ultra-light fly-fishing rod, removed the sections of graphite from their wrapping of cloth and assembled them into a pole. To the cork handle I attached my reel, then threaded tapered leader and line through the eyelets. To the end I tied a tiny, brown caddis fly and cast it onto the roiling flats. On tiny filaments of bird feather it rafted among twigs and dandelion spores over haystacks of whitewater and vanished in the foam. I set the hook, my rod arcing over my shoulder like a honing antenna, directing sight to the middle of the river where a trout splashed back into the blue-black stream. As it raced against the current, my reel whined, and when it leapt from the river a second time, I watched its entire flight from takeoff to landing. I reeled it in, a beautiful eleven-inch rainbow, and let it go without exposing its gills to the air or soiling the delicate chemistry of its skin.

We were one, that trout and I. I was one with the bison, the red-tailed hawk. I was one with the dirt in my boot treads, the sulfuric gasses bubbling from the hot spring, the cloudless sky. As I hitchhiked through Yellowstone, I was one with the vehicles in which I rode, one with their spark plugs and motor mounts, their fan belts, alternators, carburetors, and valves, as well as the vehicles that passed me by. I was one with the drivers and their passengers, and they, whether they knew it or not, were one with me. If everything was one with everything else, then none of us were stuck with who we were; like carbon atoms, which combined with other elements more readily than any other on the Periodic Table, we could be anyone or anything we wished. And as I concocted stories about myself and passed them off as the truth, I thought myself profound.

It was while backpacking a day later along the Bechler River in the southwestern corner of the park that I met Carla and Ron, recently married geneticists doing post-doctoral work at the University of Illinois at Urbana-Champaign. The first day of what would amount to a three-day hike, they passed me as I lunched on handfuls of gorp, then I passed them as they snacked on Ritz Crackers and Brie, then they passed me as I soaked in a thermal bath, and I passed them as they were setting up their tent. By then we were on a first-name basis, and Ron asked me if I wanted to set up my tent next to theirs at the backcountry campsite they had reserved.

"There's plenty of room," he said, squatting on his haunches before a tent peg.

"And we'd appreciate the company."

Carla, on all fours straightening their sleeping bags, peered out from the triangular entrance, her caramel-colored hair in braids that fell to narrow, angular wrists.

"What Ron means," she said, "is we're bored shitless by each other and could use the company."

She laughed, and I laughed, too, though Ron's full beard couldn't hide his set jaw or pained scowl. "I think I'll press on," I said. "But thanks anyway."

As I tipped my cap, Carla called, "See you tomorrow?"

"Not if I see you first," I called back.

Though Pauline hadn't been waiting for me at the Boiling River Hot Spring, I nonetheless entertained the ridiculous notion that as darkness fell she would miraculously appear at my campsite. She would have a quarter mile left to hike, and I would make the same offer to her that Ron and Carla had made to me, and as she unpacked her tent I would tell her not to bother, there was plenty of room in mine. But, of course, she didn't appear—nobody did—and when Ron and Carla passed by my campsite the next morning I was cooking three small cutthroat in papillotes of aluminum foil. Two I'd landed the night before and strung in the stream on an aspen bough, the other I'd caught and cleaned before sunrise.

When I invited them to join me for breakfast, they glanced at each other, and Ron said, "Whatever you're making smells delicious."

"Trout," I said.

As they took off their backpacks, Carla said, "I'm sure it'll beat Ron's oatmeal."

"The oatmeal wasn't that bad," Ron said. "Carla's exaggerating."

"You're right," Carla said. "I'm exaggerating. I

must've hallucinated the hole you dug with a spade as well as the lumps of oatmeal lying in it."

"I made more than we could eat," Ron said apologetically.

"Which explains why I'm so famished how?" Carla replied.

I asked them if they had their own cups, plates, and utensils, and Ron produced two sets from his backpack. As we sat on the trunks of fallen trees sipping Sanka, they asked me where I was going and where I'd been, and I told them I was on my way to Bozeman to meet up with my traveling companion Pauline, whose grandfather had passed away suddenly in Columbus, Ohio while we were hitchhiking from Big Bend National Park, where we'd spent the winter with other desert-worshipping longhairs like ourselves.

"Pauline and her granddad were very close," I said, embellishing a story told to me the summer before with details from stories told to me by drivers who'd picked me up on the plains of Minnesota and North Dakota. "Apparently they smoked a lot of weed together when she was a kid. I guess he was pretty cool for an old fart. Attending his funeral was very important to her. I couldn't talk her out of it. So we parted ways in Amarillo on our way here."

"You didn't want to accompany her to the funeral?" Carla asked.

"Of course I did," I replied. "After all the peyote buttons we ate and vision quests we went on, I would've accompanied her to hell and back. But she felt the funeral was something she had to do on her own, and ultimately I had to respect her wishes, upsetting to me as they were."

"You poor thing," Carla said.

"I miss her," I said, "but we'll be together again soon enough."

"How cool is that?" Ron said. "You two are hippies, aren't you? Real honest-to-goodness hippies."

I scratched my beard, ran my fingers through my sun-streaked locks, and in spite of the closeness of the woods pretended to ponder a distant horizon no one else could see. "I don't know about that," I said.

"No, you are," Ron exclaimed. "You're a real hippie. Know how I know?"

Carla sighed. "Oh dear God."

"How?" I asked.

"Real hippies don't know they're hippies. If you'd told me, 'Yeah, man, I'm a hippie,' I'd know you weren't. But you said you didn't know, which means you are."

"Honey," Carla said. "It's 1982. There are no hippies left. They went the way of the tyrannosaurus rex."

"Be that as it may, 'Hippie' is a term," Ron said, "coined by The Establishment. As a consequence, no self-respecting hippie would ever identify as one. To do so would constitute selling out."

"You'll have to excuse my husband," Carla said. "Until today I had no idea he was a closet sociologist."

"Breakfast's ready," I said and pulled the foil envelopes from the fire with pliers, setting one on each plate.

"Wow," Ron said.

While we ate they stopped their bickering, but when

nothing was left of the trout but heads, tails, bones, and skin, they began anew. I felt sorry for Ron. His wife was a good six inches taller than him, and I wondered if her height advantage fed her sense of entitlement. In terms of sheer physical attractiveness, they were a mismatch, and as we hiked I pictured her playing beach volleyball in a string bikini while he watched from the sidelines fanning his brow with a scorecard. Though he laughed at jokes she made at his expense and took pride in telling me of her research accomplishments in the hybridization of rot-resistant corn, you could tell by the way he clinched his teeth that he'd grown weary of her barbs. As the trail meandered across meadows of wildflowers, then through stands of ponderosa pine, I basked in their reverence, inexplicable as it was.

Back at the University of Illinois at Urbana-Champaign were colleagues upon whose sexual lives Ron and Carla speculated tirelessly, and while at first I was shocked that they would speak so frankly in front of me, a person they barely knew, I was also titillated by their conversation and liked imagining the small, incestuous clique of which they were a part. There were Marnie and Doug, Cassandra and Howard, Al and Violet, couples that might well be reconfigured or no longer configured at all by the time Ron and Carla returned from their vacation. Each person, I was given to understand, had slept at one time or another with every other person, and who knew what might happen were Doug to make a pass at Violet who had the hots for Cassandra who, in turn, had gotten over her breakup with Al but not with Marnie. That Cassandra and Howard were on the verge of breaking up themselves seemed to thrill both Ron and Carla, for Howard had taken full credit for research Ron had collaborated with him on and Cassandra, according to Carla, had said horrid things about her to Doug, who supervised the lab and could, if he wished, replace the entire team with Graduate Assistants.

"A person would need a Ph.D. to truly comprehend all the intricacies," Carla said.

"It's boring," Ron replied. "*We're* boring."

"No, you aren't," I said.

"That's sweet," Carla replied, "but married people are boring by nature, and Ron and I are no exception."

"We know how to succeed at school," Ron said, "but little else."

Carla batted her eyes in a way I thought fetching. "Ron thinks if he'd gone to Vietnam instead of getting college deferments until he was too old to be drafted, his life would be better."

"That's not true," he replied.

"Or if he'd protested the war," she said, "or supported it, taken some sort of stand, for or against—"

"Enough, Carla," he said.

"The truth is," she said, "he's jealous of you for having been born too late to have had to worry about shit like that at all."

"Really?" I said.

"Christ," she whispered, "he's jealous of me for being a woman."

That night, after a potluck of freeze-dried beef stroganoff, canned pork and beans, and three more cut-throat I'd landed to Ron and Carla's amazement and awe, I found the pint of Canadian Club I'd bought in Gardiner three nights before and made us Irish coffees. "Pauline's a very lucky woman," Carla said after one sip of my concoction. By then the three of us had christened our friendship with a naked soak and were enjoying the innocent camaraderie of people brought together by happenstance who wound up, against all odds, liking one another. The next day they would hike to the Toyota Corolla they'd left parked at the trailhead and be on their way back to the University of Illinois at Urbana-Champaign. I, on the other hand, was hitchhiking to Alaska, though were Pauline to appear and ask me to go with her back to Maine, I probably would have. Johanna didn't want me, nor did my parents, who were still furious with me for dropping out of college, a luxury for which I might've paid dearly ten years before.

"So are you, Carla," I said, "and, Ron, you're a very lucky man."

"We're going to miss you," Carla said.

"You've brought us closer together," Ron said, and Carla didn't disagree.

That night we sipped whiskey and told stories around the campfire, theirs told by them both with one supplying what the other omitted and in corroborating each other eliminating any doubt as to their stories' veracity. Though mine were entirely fictitious and tried credibility at every turn, neither Ron nor Carla issued a word of protest. Indeed, as I told them about the encampment beside the Rio Grande and the orgy Pauline and I had participated in, they were as rapt as children of Hamlin.

"It was on the night of the vernal equinox," I said. "And while Pauline and I were making our weekly run into Boquias for peyote and mescal, the others were applying clay to their faces and weaving elaborate masks from creosotebush and thistle, such that when we returned after midnight tripping and drunk, more than a hundred naked revelers were conjoined on the ground, squirming and groaning, their bodies shimmering like ivory in the moonlight."

"Why the masks and clay?" Ron asked.

"An orgy," Carla said as if speaking to a child, "isn't about who you are or how you look. It isn't about identity or personality. In an orgy everyone's equal, isn't that right?"

"That's right," I said. "A face only matters in so far as it contains a mouth to suck with and a tongue to lick with."

"In an orgy everyone's just a body," Carla said, "and that's what's so great about them. The self, or ego, is squashed, obliterated."

"Sent to Kingdom Come," I said, which made Carla laugh. Though I could see Ron didn't abide the direction the conversation had taken and of the two of them I liked him more, having begun my story I couldn't stop it, caught as I was between allures: a vision of epic carnality as vivid as anything I'd ever actually experienced and an attractive listener aroused by what I was painting in her mind with words. "Bodies lay strewn over a hundred square yards," I said, "and from this quivering, moaning carpet of humanity rose picnic tables, tents, and cottonwood trees. It looked like a massive battlefield of limbs and torsos, genitals and breasts, fingers, toes, and buttocks, to pleasure or be pleasured each body part's only purpose."

"So what did you do?" Carla asked as Ron grew ever more contemplative and tense. "I presume you and Pauline joined in the festivities."

"We did," I said, "but once we shed what little we were wearing and smeared clay across each other's cheeks and foreheads, a strange thing happened. We were tripping, right?"

"Uh-huh," Carla said.

"Well, no sooner had we applied the clay than we became two-dimensional."

"Weird," Carla said.

"When Pauline turned to the side, she vanished. And when I turned to the side, I became invisible to her. 'If we go in there,' I said to Pauline, 'we might never find each other again.'"

"But she wanted to anyway, right?"

"She did," I replied, "and I did, too. But we were as frightened as little children."

"What did you do?"

"Facing each other, we knelt beside the orgy, and as the orgy lapped against the backs of our calves and the soles of our feet, I said, 'On the count of three, we're going to fully immerse ourselves. Are you ready?' Pauline nodded. 'OK,' I said, and when I'd counted to three, we turned to the orgy and entered it."

"What was it like?" Carla asked. "Was it everything you thought it would be?"

I scratched my head. "It was as if I had fallen into the sea," I said, "and were being carried away by currents and, at the same time, as if I were soaring through space and all around me were planets and stars."

"Jesus," Carla said.

"It was a trip," I said, "a real trip."

Her smile flickered in the glow of our campfire, and though I could see that I'd succeeded in touching something deep within her, I didn't want it to be at Ron's expense. So when he yawned and told us he was turning in, in effect leaving his wife to me, I said I would do the same and for this kindness received nary a wink of gratitude.

Carla remained seated before the campfire, and through the mosquito netting of my tent I watched her. Was she waiting for me? And if I joined her what exactly would we consummate?

In time she picked her way over twigs to the tent she shared with her husband and soon they were fucking, and a little after that Ron called out, "You still up?"

"Who? Me?" I called back.

"Yeah you," he replied.

"Yeah, I'm still up."

"You want to join us?"

"Really?" I said.

"Uh-huh," he said.

Twigs snapped under my feet as I crept nude across the campsite to their tent. In the dim light of our campfire, it looked like a jack-o-lantern whose candle had died, its cutout mouth and eyes darkened. "I'm here," I said, and the mosquito netting unzipped and fell back into the opening like gauze, and there they lay side by side on top of their sleeping bags, Ron's penis resting on his wife's thigh like a thing detached. As I slipped in beside her, he reached across both of us and zipped the mosquito netting shut.

"You want to fuck her? Be my guest." When I looked to Ron for confirmation that he'd actually meant what he'd just said, he nodded. "Don't worry. Everything's cool."

"You're sure?" I said for Carla's lids were closed and she looked as if she might be sleeping.

"You'd be doing us a favor," Ron said. "Bringing us closer together."

When I climbed on top of her, Carla parted her legs, and no sooner had I put myself inside her than she thrust her pelvis into mine and began to moan. "That means she wants to be fucked hard," Ron said, coaching me, his palm moist against the small of my back. "When she moans like that you have to fuck her hard." I thrust into her as hard as I thought reasonable and looked to Ron for approval. "Harder, man. You have to fuck her like you hate her, like you really hate her." As I thrust into her harder and harder, Ron kept saying, "Harder, man. You have to fuck her like you hate her, like you really hate her," but I couldn't, and finally Ron said, "Get off of her and I'll show you."

So I rolled off of her, and as I lay beside her Ron thrust into her so hard I thought the wall would rip from the floor as the pegs pulled from the earth and

214

soon poles and nylon would collapse upon us. But they didn't. "You see? Like this," he said above Carla's moaning. "You like it like this, don't you, baby? Don't you? You see? This is how she likes it, don't you, baby? Watch and learn, my friend."

I sympathized with Ron. He was doing this for her, and as he spoke to us both in turn his expression oscillated from hatred to its opposite, such that once he was lying on top of her and pumping her straight into the ground, he turned to me, and in the silvered darkness I saw heartache etched into his brow. I kissed him then. I didn't think about it, I just did it, such that the whiskers of our beards entwined and when he jerked away it felt as if a bandage had been torn from my lips.

"Oh God," he said. "Oh God, oh God, oh God." Cowering in a corner of the tent, he cupped his genitals as if blighted. "I should kill you for doing that," he said. "I should kill you."

"Hey, what's going on?" Carla asked, sitting upright in the center of the tent, her breasts weighted as if by stones.

"What he just did to me," Ron said, "was so awful, so awful—" He held his face in his hands and rebuffed her efforts to console him. "Don't touch me," he said. "I don't want to be touched until he, if that's even what *he* is, until *that* thing, that piece of detritus, that walking, talking fungal infection, that—"

It was no use springing on him my theory of the carbon atom, something I was sure he understood far better than I. "I'm leaving," I said, unzipped the mosquito netting and crawled out onto the dirt. The fact was, I was not yet twenty and didn't know myself well enough to know if what I'd done meant anything, everything, or nothing at all.

"If you're here in the morning I'll kill you," Ron said. "Indeed I might have to kill you both."

By then our campfire was glowing embers, and as I thought about the part of my story I'd intentionally left out, the morning after the orgy when I'd arisen at dawn and searched among the bodies for my love, I couldn't decide which I felt sorrier for, the 'me' I'd made up or the 'me' I was.

Daniel Mueller is the author of *How Animals Mate*, which won the Sewanee Fiction Prize. He is the grateful recipient of fellowships from the National Endowment for the Arts, Massachusetts Cultural Council, and Fine Arts Work Center in Provincetown. He directs the creative writing program at the University of New Mexico and teaches on the faculty of the Low-Residency MFA Program at Queens University of Charlotte. He lives in Albuquerque.

CPSIA information can be obtained at www.ICGtesting.com
Printed in the USA
LVOW061907030213

318346LV00003B/17/P